Coronel

a novella

Stierlitz

by

Robin
Wyatt
Dunn

Published by

John Ott

San Diego,
California

ISBN:
1-940830-14-8

for

Basia

Part 1
Moscow

Stierlitz opened a door. The lights went on. Stierlitz closed the door. The lights went out. Stierlitz opened the door again. The light went back on. Stierlitz closed the door. The light went out again.

"I'm a refrigerator," concluded Stierlitz.

-- traditional Russian joke

Colonel Stierlitz eyes the microphone.

This will be the last time I do this, he thinks.

"Is the Soviet propaganda machine on?" he asks the microphone.

"Yes, I'm on," the microphone says.

"This is Colonel Stierlitz here," says Colonel Stierlitz.

"Go on," says the microphone.

"Please be quiet microphone," says Colonel Stierlitz.

"All right," says the microphone.

"I have something to say. I've been asleep for a long time," says Colonel Stierlitz.

"We know, Stierlitz," says the microphone.

"Please be quiet," says Stierlitz. "I know I should have woken up sooner. But anyway, now I'm awake. And I have something to say. I believe I understand what's happened. In my dream, I was a horse. And I was riding on the steppes. In my dream as a horse, I encountered Genghis Khan, and I greeted him, neighing dramatically. Genghis smiled at me, and I ran, over the fields, into the marsh, where I nearly drowned. But I escaped, with the help of a small gnome."

"A gnome, Stierlitz?" says the microphone.

"Yes, a gnome. He helped me to escape."

"Stierlitz," says the microphone, "Why are you telling this story?"

"In my dream,' says Stierlitz, "Genghis loved me. He rode me over the long fields, holding tight to my mane. I loved him. When I awoke, I found myself here in this cell, and I wept."

"We saw you weeping," says the microphone.

"That is another matter," says Stierlitz. "Tell me. Have you been a microphone for long?"

"Not very long," says the microphone.

"You're good at what you do," says Stierlitz.

"Thank you," says the microphone.

"Tell me," says Stierlitz. "Do you have any vodka?"

"No," says the microphone.

"None at all?"

"Well, I was saving it."

"I understand," says Stierlitz. "How about we share it?"

"All right," says the microphone. "It's a secret compartment under your bed."

Stierlitz opened the secret compartment and took out the bottle of vodka. He poured some of it over the microphone.

"Mmm," says the microphone.

Stierlitz put the vodka next to the microphone.

"I knew your mother," says Stierlitz. He poured more vodka over the microphone.

The microphone made a small sound.

"She was a good woman. Tell me, microphone, where is the key to my door?"

"Inside me," says the microphone.

Stierlitz opens the microphone and takes out the small key.

"You're a good microphone," says Stierlitz.

"I'm bad. Terrible," says the microphone.

Stierlitz opened the door and let himself out.

Stierlitz inhaled the air of the fields. It was Moscow, and he was in Red Square, but it was the fields.

He went to his favorite bar and ordered vodka.

"Stierlitz. Fighting for the country?" asked the barman.

"Yes," sais Stierlitz. "I am."

"How is your family?" asked the barman.

"They are asleep," said Stierlitz.

"Vodka," said the barman, and he poured. Stierlitz drank.

"More please," said Stierlitz.

"Last night there was rain," said the barman. Stierlitz listened.

"I heard a horse."

"What kind of horse?" asked Stierlitz.

"A hussar's horse," said the barman.

"He was big, was he?" asked Stierlitz.

"Yes, obviously," said the barman.

"How big was he?" asked Stierlitz.

The barman looked at Colonel Stierlitz.

Stierlitz looked away. He looked out the door, at the Russian dusk.

"Colonel, are you all right?" asked the barman.

"I've been dreaming," said the colonel.

"More vodka?" asked the barman.

"No thank you," said Stierlitz. He thanked the bartender and walked outside.

In the light, he felt at peace. He walked home, and went to sleep, next to his wife.

Stierlitz slept for a very long time. All day, and all night. When he awoke, it was dark outside, and he went outside, to smoke a cigarette. The lights from the Kremlin were low, and red.

He lit the cigarette and inhaled, watching the dawn approach his house.

In his dream, he had been a horse again, but with no rider. He had been alone, in the steppes. He had felt very quiet.

Slowly the sun rose, and Stierlitz poured himself some vodka, which he drank quickly, then putting on his boots and his coat.

In the street, the ice-salesman saluted him, and he clapped the man on the shoulder, heading down to the cafe.

He ate his favorite lunch, veal, and eel. With a light German beer.

The men came over and he told jokes with them. Outside, a young woman was sitting, texting into her cel phone.

Stierlitz went outside to speak with her.

"Good morning, lovely," he said.

"Hmm," she said, texting into her phone.

"What is your name?" asked Colonel Stierlitz.

She did not answer, but continued to text into her phone.

"Am I disturbing you?" asked the Colonel.

"One moment," the young woman said.

The Colonel watched the young woman type into her phone. She had delicate fingers which she poised over its shining screen.

"What is it you want?" asked the young woman.

"Only to know your name," said Stierlitz.

"Ekaterina," she said.

"A beautiful name," said the colonel. "I had a grandmother named Ekaterina."

"No one cares who she was now," said the young woman.

"What do you mean? What are you trying to say?" asked Stierlitz.

The young woman put away her phone and stood up.

"You are with the intelligence services?" she asked.

"I am," said Stierlitz.

"You claim to serve the Motherland?" she said.

"I do," said Stierlitz.

"Always politics with you!" the woman said. She sounded emotional.

"Not only that," said Stierlitz. "It is love."

"No!" said the young woman, and she ran from the cafe.

Colonel Stierlitz raised his hand to his nose, and watched the young woman run from him. He walked from the cafe then, putting his hands in his pockets.

Above them, the sun had peeked from behind the clouds.

"What are your hands doing in your pockets?" said a policeman.

"Fuck off," said Stierlitz.

★

The next morning a solider in the Red Guard interrupted Colonel Stierlitz's breakfast.

"Max, we have revivified Stalin," the soldier said.

The Colonel stood and placed his napkin back on his breakfast table.

"When did you do this?"

"Just now."

"We must kill him."

"I know," said the soldier.

"Where is he now?"

"On parade."

"Is your weapon loaded?" asked Stierlitz.

"Yes."

"Give it to me."

Stierlitz went out on his balcony. Below was the parade. Stalin was there, at the front, a walking corpse. Stierlitz took aim carefully, and shot the corpse in the head. Part of the skull exploded, but the body kept walking. He took aim at the legs instead. One shot in one knee, and one in the other, and Stalin was down.

The parade marched over Stalin. Stierlitz wiped his nose.

"It's cold out," he remarked.

The solider nodded.

"We must burn the corpse," Stierlitz said.

"Don't trouble yourself, Max. It's taken care of."

Stierlitz nodded.

"Max, that Stalin. Was he real?" asked the soldier.

"You revivified him, didn't you?"

"Yes. You're a good man, Max. Where would we be without you?"

"Soldier, I'll buy you some food. Let's go."

They walked down to the cafe. People were talking about the shooting.

"They've killed Stalin again!" one woman remarked.

Colonel Stierlitz found he couldn't digest his food. He excused himself from the solider and began to walk down the road.

By a tree, he sat, and looked at the sky. It was a beautiful morning.

He saw the young woman from the other day. He tried to stand but found his legs had stiffened.

"Lady Ekaterina! I would stand, but I find that..."

"Don't trouble yourself, Colonel. I can do enough standing for the two of us."

"Thank you."

"I am going to sell my family jewels today," said the young woman.

"For rubles?" asked the Colonel.

The young woman laughed. "No, dollars."

"Oh," said the Colonel. "Is everything all right?"

"Oh, yes, fine. We're just bankrupt, that's all."

The Colonel tried to stand again. The young woman bent down beside him, her cheek very close to his face.

"Please, Colonel, don't trouble yourself."

"Your phone, where is it?" hissed the Colonel.

"What?"

"Your phone. Turn if off at once."

The young woman did as she was told.

"Help me up."

She balanced against the tree, and placed both hands around Stierlitz's.

"Unnh."

She lifted him up.

"Thank you," said Stierlitz. "Your family. Are they asleep?"

"Asleep now? Now, they're awake now. Colonel, are you all right?"

"Take me back to my apartment."

"Call for a taxi for all I care! I shouldn't have stopped anyway!"

"Please," said the Colonel, placing his hand on her shoulder.

Stiffly, she offered her arm to him, and he took it. They walked back north, along the road.

"I am a married man. I suffer for it," said the Colonel.

"You are fortunate."

"Yes."

"Today I will kill myself," the young woman announced.

"A good day for it," agreed Stierltiz.

"I shall hang."

"Enough of that," said the Colonel. "Let's get drunk."

9

And they did.

Later that night, Stierlitz remarked that she was a very beautiful woman, and she cackled like an old hag. They were both very drunk. The lights in the bar were gloomy and dark, full of beauty. He embraced her and kissed her, tasting the alcohol.

"You are a madman, Stierlitz. You are a service to your country."

"My country is shit!" announced Stierltiz, very drunk now. The bartender, an old man at the bar in a large hat, and an old, thin woman in grey watched the Colonel as he shouted. "My country is shit country!" He laughed. Ekaterina laughed too.

The thin old woman handed Stierlitz a note. It read "Come at once. The Kremlin."

Stierlitz stood, on rickety legs.

"I must go."

"Don't," said Ekaterina.

"I will see you later, sweet," he said, and kissed her on the cheek.

Outside, it was very cold. He made his way across Red Square to the Kremlin. Inside, Stalin sat atop his throne. His face bore many stitches.

"You shot me earlier today Comrade," said Stalin.

"I am not your Comrade, Comrade Stalin. And I'm sorry I shot you. But you were dead. Are dead." Colonel Stierlitz looked in his pocket for his pistol and found it missing. That damned Ekaterina! She had lifted it!

"And now I find my mistress has lifted my pistol!"

"Enough about your mistress, Colonel. We have business to discuss."

The Colonel sat in the chair near Stalin's throne, listening, still very drunk.

"I want to buy a bakery," said Stalin.

"Oh?" said the Colonel.

"Will you help me?"

"Do you have any vodka?" asked Stierlitz.

"Yes, of course," said Stalin, taking a small metal flask from inside his jacket. He handed it to the Colonel.

"Thank you," said Stierlitz, and drank. "I must tell you, I know nothing about bakeries."

"Neither do I," said Stalin. "But I want one."

"Very well. I will see what I can do." Stierlitz looked in his pocket again, the remembered the pistol was gone. He would have to shoot Stalin again later. The man would not stay dead.

Out in the cold, Stierlitz found a musician playing his fiddle, to a very merry tune, and they danced in the freezing cold together, sharing Stalin's vodka.

He sang an ancient Russian song, from before Russians were Russians. Only people living in the freezing cold of the steppe, before the Vikings had come.

As he danced, he saw mist rising over Red Square.

"My dear musician, we must escape this mist," Stierlitz said. The musician agreed. They walked, arm in arm, back to Stierlitz's apartment.

Stierlitz put the musician on the couch, and returned to his bed, where he lay down next to his wife. She was still asleep.

In the morning, Stierltiz shaved, showered and breakfasted on kippered herring, English style. Then he sat at his desk and dialed the operator.

"Get me the bakery," said Stierltiz.

The phone was ringing.

"Yes?" said the baker.

"Stalin wants to buy you," Stierltiz said.

"Is that code for something?" the baker asked, in his gravel voice.

"No. How much do you want for the place?"

"I'm not selling!" said the baker, and hung up.

Colonel Stierlitz wiped his chin. He found that sweat collected there. Outside in the Square, little girls were playing tag. He stood a moment to watch them through the window. His own daughter was still asleep. He stretched the blanket over her and went out into the day.

Outside, he saw a news van and began to run at once.

He ran into the bar. The same people were sitting there from before. Quickly, Stierlitz borrowed the hat from the old man and put it on his head.

"There is a news van out there," said Stierlitz.

"That is my hat on your head," said the old man.

"Yes," said Stierlitz.

"You are with the intelligence services."

"Yes," agreed Stierlitz.

"I have information for you."

"What is your name?"

"I am Eliza. I am forty-seven years old."

"You look eighty if you're a day. What is your patronymic?"

"It is Denisovich."

"You're a traitor."

"A patriot, Colonel. Will you listen to my information?"

"All right." Stierlitz thought about asking for vodka but he had begun to feel ill.

"My daughter is having a celebration this evening. She would like you to be there."

"Your daughter? I'm sorry, I haven't had the pleasure ..."

"My daughter's name is Ekaterina. You are acquainted with her."

The Colonel's face grew red. He pulled the hat down tighter over his ears, and looked out the window of the bar to see if the news van had gone away.

"You will come to the party tonight, Vsevolod Vladimirovich Vladimirov."

"You know my name?" asked the Colonel, astonished.

"I know many things about you. It is casual dress, but you may dress up if it pleases you. I don't see why you insist on wearing that uniform everywhere, anyway. Will you come?"

"Of course."

The old man excused himself from the bar. Stierlitz was still wearing the old man's hat. He looked again for the news van. It had gone. He stepped into the street.

Some of the little girls were still playing tag in Red Square, and Stierlitz went to watch them. He leaned against the statue of Dostoyevsky and watched their play. Overhead, the sun had gone behind the clouds. It was very cold.

Suddenly the Colonel remembered: he had been arrested. He had been imprisoned. The microphone, and his close escape. Who had arrested him?

Stierlitz approached the little girl in white.

"Do you know who arrested me, little girl?" he asked her.

"It was Stalin!" said the little girl.

"No, he was dead. Who could it have been?"

"You're on duty, Vsevolod Vladimirovich Vladimirov. But I am a little girl and would like to play."

"Of course. Please excuse me." The Colonel bowed to the little girl and she bowed back.

The Colonel made his way to the Kremlin.

"Something isn't right here," thought Colonel Stierlitz. "Russia has changed."

The guards let him in to the palace but Stalin was nowhere to be found.

"Where is Stalin?" he asked the guard.

"He is walking," said the guard.

"I seem to have forgotten my pistol," said Stierltiz. "May I borrow yours?"

"No," said the guard.

"Have a fine day!" said the Colonel, through clenched teeth.

The guard nodded.

Outside, it had begun to rain. It was freezing cold rain. In a moment it would be hail. The Colonel thought about running through the rain, straight home, to confess all his fears and shames to his wife, asleep on their bed. He felt ashamed of this childish urge, and straightened his coat.

He turned on his cel phone and called his mistress.

"I'll be there tonight," he said.

"Don't be late! It's my special day!"

"You're killing yourself, aren't you?" the Colonel asked, suddenly realizing the occasion.

"Of course not! Don't be silly. It's only a nice party. I've decided to call it a Flower Party. Even though no flowers are in season now. Tell me, Maxy, will you bring me flowers?"

"Of course shnookums." He hung up. He was beginning to realize he had a very peculiar mistress. In his mind he could visualize her perfect calves. And the curve of her hipbone.

The hail had begun to fall. His friend the crow swooped onto his shoulder then.

"Odin," said the crow.

"Crow," said Max.

"Kraak!"

They stood in the rain together, under the eave.

Red Square was beautiful: dark grey, and light grey.

Above, they could begin to see the stars.

"Kraak!" said the crow.

"Kraak!" agreed Colonel Stierlitz.

The crow flew away. The Colonel waved goodbye to it. He turned off his phone and began to make his way to the party, hunting for any dandelions along the way. He had forgotten his umbrella.

Once when Colonel Stierlitz was very young he had had a dream of Russia. The Viking Russia, blonde, and white. He had dreamt he was a Viking ship from Kiev, fighting into the steppe. His body had split the Volga's waters like an axe does a tree. In the dream, he had waited for the Vikings to return, lying in the cold waters. Finally they did, bringing a woman slave with them. She was tied up, in the bottom of the boat, and she whispered against the calked boards that were Stierlitz: "You are Colonel Stierlitz" in a quiet, strong voice. And as a little boy, Max knew on waking that he would enter the army when he was grown.

Outside Ekaterina's apartment, Stierlitz was soaking wet. He still had the old man's stovepipe hat on his head. He rang the bell.

"Maxy! You're soaked! Oh my God! Come in at

once!"

She hauled her man into her apartment, which was filled with candlelight.

She stripped him of his clothing, and he stood there shivering.

"I know why your family is asleep," Ekaterina said, looking straight at him.

"Why are they?"

"It's because of you, Max."

"What did I do?"

"What didn't you do. Come, into the bath."

She lay him in hot water, and scrubbed his fattening body.

"Ekaterina I love you," he whispered.

"Shh," she said. She dried his hair, then drained the bath. She removed her robe.

"I am going to have your child. But first you must fuck me."

"What about the party?" Max asked.

She kissed him.

Max lay satiated on the settee. Around him the literati were discussing books and literary journals, while they ate olives. Max had put the one dandelion he'd found on the street in Ekaterina's hair. She looked beautiful. Ekaterina came from a name meaning "human sacrifice," or, perhaps, "torturer." A very Russian name. (Though it comes from Armenia).

Max ate little, but sipped his vodka. He smiled

when people talked to him, and listened. It was a fine Flower Party.

Overhead, the chandelier was lit with real candles. They dripped, fitfully, and the guests dodged the hot wax.

Max lifted his phone and spoke into the receiver.

"I'm going to kill you again Stalin."

The guests listened attentively.

"He's drunk again," whispered Ekaterina.

"It was you who arrested me!" Max was standing now, shouting into his phone. "You no good thug!"

"Enough Maxy!" Ekaterina announced. "No more phone for you tonight." She took the cel phone away from me.

"I want my gun back!" shouted Max.

"I'm going to kill myself with it!" she shouted back.

The guests laughed. They were a sweet couple.

"I want you to myself," Max whispered to his mistress, after the party had died down.

"We have business to discuss," she said.

"Not again!" said Max.

"We've never discussed business before. Well, aside from my confession about the bankruptcy. And you were very helpful with that. This is different. It affects Mother Russia."

"Tell me."

"Well, when I was a little girl I used to live in the forest."

"In the forest? Surely not." Max touched her arm, and watched her face, adoring her.

"Yes, in the forest. I was a little forest girl. I learned the mushrooms and the bees and the seasons, like a little Cro-Magnon. When I was old enough my mother sent me to school, where I learned to read and write Russian. It's not my first language, you know."

"It's not?"

"No, silly. My language only has maybe, hmm, sixty speakers left now. We're dying. Bankrupt, and dying! Ha ha ha!"

"Don't kill yourself, darling."

"Not today, anyway. I need your help."

But Stierlitz had already fallen asleep.

Max remarked to the doctor: "You missed a spot by his nose. The bone is showing."

"He won't miss it," said the doctor, smiling.

"Cover it up," said Max. The doctor did so spreading the rubber with makeup over the skeleton.

"He's almost ready," said the doctor.

"He looks disgusting."

"He's not so bad."

"This man should stay dead."

"Not my responsibility."

"But it is. You're bringing him back to life."

"And what of what we can learn from him? The afterlife."

"It remains a mystery. I'm telling you doctor, this is the last time. If you bring him back to life again, I will shoot him, and then shoot you."

"Very well," said the doctor, and connected the electrodes. Stierlitz watched as the corpse screamed itself to life.

The doctor detached the electrodes, and left the laboratory. Stalin sat up.

"How is the bakery coming?" Stalin asked.

"Very well. Listen, I—" His gun was still missing from his pocket. He had put it back in his pocket after the first time, he's lectured Ekaterina about it. He knew he had. Had Ekaterina taken it from him again? She knew he needed it to protect his life.

Stalin saw Max's hand in his pocket and attacked.

The living corpse knocked the Colonel to the ground. Over him Stierlitz could smell the putrefying flesh. He jabbed his fist into the side of Stalin's head. The corpse howled, and stood, disoriented.

Stalin fled the laboratory, moving faster than Stierlitz had ever seen him.

To serve the Motherland was to undergo danger, as a matter of course. The challenge was to remember the land itself. If something was good for the land, it was good for the Colonel. To kill an abomination—even Comrade Stalin—was to please the Motherland.

This was why the Colonel did not like to talk

politics. It confused the issue. The land itself was holy. All other considerations were dross.

He took his time climbing the stairs back to Red Square. If his family were still asleep next week, he would have to put them in a home. Otherwise they would develop bed sores. The thought filled him with a terrible guilt, and a longing for Ekaterina.

Outside, the musician stood, tuning his instrument. The two men embraced.

"Stalin is alive again," said Max.

"He is cursed," said the musician.

"How is your family?" asked Max.

"Well, thank God."

"Thank God. Thank God. See you, man."

"Take care out there, Stierlitz. This winter is one motherfucker."

Stierlitz retraced his steps to the site of his last arrest. Slowly the details came back to him: the beating the Red Guard had given him, and the soup they'd fed him later, with an apology. Then a visit from his superior officer, Semyonov. Semyonov had told him there was a plot to overthrow Mother Russia's government. The Swedes were behind it, along with the Finns. Stierlitz knew this was a lie. He had listened carefully to Semyonov: what was the man trying to tell him? A man who reminded Stierlitz of his old, deaf uncle. A crafty son of a bitch he had been, imprisoned in his own dacha, and still able to plot coups. Semyonov's face had flickered in the dim light. The man was sober, Stierlitz had realized. Semyonov had stopped drinking. Then Stierlitz had woken up with the microphone in the cell.

"My boss is a teetotaler," Stierlitz said out loud. A man nearby on the street overheard, and crossed himself.

Stierlitz stopped outside the grey apartment building. Here, in the basement was where he had been held. He rang the bell.

"Colonel Stierlitz," said the concierge.

"Show me to the basement, please," said the Colonel.

"Back already?" remarked the concierge. She lit the lantern and showed him down the steps. She unlocked the cell and gestured for him to enter it. He did so, and she locked it behind him. Solemnly, Stierlitz lay his fingers on the bars.

I must have arrested myself, he thought. *But where did the microphone go? And is the vodka still under the bedding?*

The vodka was, but there wasn't much left. Stierlitz swallowed it thoughtfully, looking around the room.

Why would I have arrested myself? What didn't I want me to know?

He called for the concierge.

"Finished, Colonel?"

"I am."

She unlocked the cell and let him out.

"Madam, have you had any new tenants this year?"

"This year? No, no. But last year there were. Two young men. From America. I had them on the fourth floor. You remember them."

"No, I don't. But never mind. Listen, if I ask again, don't let me down here, will you? I seem to be going in circles."

"Whatever you say Colonel. You're the boss."

"For the moment," said Colonel Stierlitz.

He knelt beside his wife, crying.

"Please wake," he said.

But she slept on.

His mistress had asked him to do something. He had decided he could not stand to have his wife and children moved to a home, so he had hired an attendant at great expense to come to his home and clean and bathe them.

He hired a cab then, and paid the driver off so he could drive it himself. He picked Ekaterina up off the street, ignoring her protestations that she had a hair appointment.

"We're going to the country," he announced.

"But my hair! It will be ruined in the wind!" But she curled against Max's arm, holding him as he drove.

2
The Country

Stierlitz, wake up!
She was shaking his arm. The young woman.
Maxy!

Outside it was snowing. He had taken Ekaterina to his dacha. All the dachas were deserted; it was midwinter. It had taken him the damnedest time to get the flue unfrozen and a fire lit in the fireplace. He had feared they might freeze. Luckily his wood was fully supplied and they held each other all night, shivering, by the fire. Her lips were like blood, beautiful.

Now she was gone.

"Ekaterina!" he shouted into the snow.

"Over here Max!" she shouted back. He could barely see her, in a snowdrift, by the tree.

"You'll catch cold! It's freezing!"

"Come!" she shouted.

"I found mushrooms!" she said, smiling, when he got to her by the tree.

"You and your mushrooms," he said. "You could die out here."

"I'm a forest girl, remember?"

"Come inside, at once."

"Yes, papa."

"Hmmph."

He put his coat over her shoulders and listened as she cooed over the mushrooms.

"Aren't they beautiful?"

"Hmm."

Back inside, he put another log on the fire.

"I overslept," he said.

"You needed it. You drove all night. The phones aren't working."

"Not surprising. It's midwinter."

"Let's cook the mushrooms."

Colonel Stierlitz stroked her hair away from her face.

"You're beautiful," he said.

"I'll make us tea."

"It's good the phones aren't working, isn't it."

"Did you dream last night?" she asked.

"No."

"I did."

"Mm."

Stierlitz sat in his big chair. To feel the room warm up was wonderful.

"I dreamt of you."

"You're a little drug addict, aren't you," he said. She was dropping the mushrooms into the tea pot.

"I'm a witch," she said.

"Yes." Stierlitz yawned.

She came and sat his lap, watching the teapot over the fire. "Do you love me?' she asked.

"Mm."

"My mother would never forgive me. Running away with a spy like you."

"Mm."

"Do you spy in dreams, Max?"

"Sometimes."

"Do you die in dreams?"

"No. Though I've thought I might."

"Here, it's done!" she said, taking the pot off the fire.

Suddenly it seemed the day had already been very long.

Ekaterina poured from the samovar.

And they drank.

Semyonov was shouting. In the snow. Stierlitz knew it was the ghost of Semyonov. But this did not make the man any less loud.

Come outside at once! We are being invaded!

"I'm coming," mumbled Stierlitz. Kat lay sleeping in his arms, her soft skin fragrant and feline.

You must pretend to be hussar! A traitor to the czar! Tell the Swedes you are here to help them!

"They won't believe me," mumbled Stierlitz.

You must tell them. And give them the amulet! They will believe you once you give them the amulet!

"Mm," mumbled Stierlitz.

It was dark. They had eaten nothing. Stierlitz's stomach growled. He heated some kasha in the pot. Kat watched him from the bed of furs, her eyes dark.

They ate the porridge in bed, then slept again.

In the morning the car arrived from the Kremlin.

"Russia has fallen to Sweden!" the man said. He was a Swede himself; blue eyed and fair-haired.

"What is your name?" asked Colonel Stierlitz. "Please, come inside. You can call me Max. This is my wife Ekaterina."

The Swede dusted off his mittens, stepping into the dacha.

"What a beautiful wife you have!"

"And hands to yourself, thank you," said Max.

The Swede laughed, then offered his hand.

"I'm Axel."

Stierlitz took out his pistol and pointed it at the man's stomach.

"Please, sit," said Max.

Carefully, the man sat at the kitchen table. Ekaterina poured the Swede some of her tea. He sipped it.

Max sat across from the Swede and placed his gun on the edge of the table.

"Woman, search his pockets."

She stepped behind the Swede and reached into his pockets. She tossed his passport and another paper onto the table.

"My dream told me I was to offer you an amulet," said Stierlitz.

"That's not necessary," said the Swede.

"Oh, but it is. If you have truly taken the Kremlin, my dream is realized. I must swear allegiance to your king."

"Sweden is a democracy."

"Forgive me, to your democracy. But first, I would have you prove to me that the Kremlin is fallen. How can I believe this? The Rus has stood these 1300 years. Surely it would have stood another thousand or so yet!"

"That paper," said Axel, "is a signed abdication by Comrade Stalin."

Stierlitz burst out laughing.

"I should shoot you right now," said Max, taking hold of his gun but leaving it on the table. "Are you really so stupid?"

"Read it," said the Swede.

"Read it for us, darling," said Max.

Ekaterina unfolded the paper. "Drink your tea there, Axel. It's medicinal."

The Swede sipped his tea.

"The Georgian Mountains are my home, and to them I must now return. To that end, I surrender all powers generously granted to me by the Russian Motherland. Younger hands must now fight her battles. I am old, and long only for the smell of my home country. Signed, Comrade Stalin."

"It is a forgery," said Stierlitz. "Ridiculous."

"It is in his handwriting," said Axel.

"Look at it," said Kat.

Max leaned forward, examining the paper.

"Hmm. Well, Stalin is a zombie in any case. Get him drunk enough and he'll write anything. The strength of the Russian state is in its people, Herr Viking. Surely you know that. We cannot be defeated."

"I know, Stierlitz, that's why I'm here. I need your help to overthrow the Russian state, to serve the land. With Stalin on our side, we can do so. You can convince him to work with us."

"Why would Stalin do that? If you believe his letter, he is ready to retire. And about time too."

At this point Axel looked out the window of the dacha towards his automobile.

"If you will permit me," he said, "I have brought a gift."

"Go get it then," said Stierlitz. "But leave your keys here."

"He may have a gun in the car, Max. Use your head."

"You're right of course. What present have you brought us, Viking?"

"Your mother," said Axel.

His mother was very drunk as they took her out of the trunk of Axel's car.

"I need a drink," she said.

"Come inside, mother, it's cold."

They went inside and drank the last of the tea.

"There's an assignment for you in America," his mother said.

"Russia needs me, mother," said Stierlitz.

"Russia needs you in America now."

"We can spare you for a few months, Stierlitz," said Axel.

"I don't work for you!" shouted Stierlitz.

"You are, Vsevolod. You love your mother. Go to America. There's a good boy."

"I'm not your little boy anymore, mother."

"You'll always be my little boy."

Ekaterina poured the last drops of tea. Mother slurped them up, greedily. Ekaterina handed her a napkin.

Alex put his ticket on the table.

"Goddamn it," said Stierlitz.

"We're going to America!" shouted Ekaterina.

3
America

The flight was wonderful; all you could drink. Ekaterina was on her third bottle of California Chardonnay.

Outside the plane window, Colonel Stierlitz watched the snow fall on the Alps. Connection in London, then New York, then Los Angeles, then Long Beach.

Stierlitz closed his eyes. Behind his eyes he felt the rhythm of the cosmos, and he felt the presence of the gnome who had saved him on the dream Russian steppe. The gnome smiled inside his mind, and Stierlitz smiled a little too, a twitch in his mouth. Ekaterina stuck her drunk tongue into his ear and he smiled wider.

Night in Long Beach was like night in Moscow, a crowd of lonely people watching one another. Paranoia, a fine after dinner drink for a Muscovite, was in southern California more of an appetizer; a beginning rather than an ending. Stierlitz's Russian eyes scanned the crowd as Ekaterina swayed her beautiful hips to the music.

To protect Mother Russia one must do many things, Stierlitz knew. As long as one knew that one served Mother Russia—her soil and the soil's blessings—one could do anything. In his weakest moments, Stierlitz might... but no. He knew what it was to serve the land. It meant to die inside. From inside his cold Russian eyes Colonel Stierlitz knew a love shared by all Russians. His privilege was to be able to give expression to that love with action.

His task now was to listen to the music and to watch the crowd. He did this.

On stage the young man pranced around, shaking his long hair. The huge speaker system pounded the air, trembling Max's heart. Ekaterina swirled, dodging the drunk revelers around her. Colored lights flashed down into the crowd, the street party.

The question Stierlitz needed to answer was: What did America want?

This was Long Beach, a suburb of Los Angeles, its chief port, part of the physical strucure of the dream machine of Hollywood, one of the places where the desires of this North American nation were built, sanded, soldered, shipped, and sold to the people. On stage the people's dreams were bonded through the young body of the singer, singing about himself—typical American style, this, songs of the self, rather than songs of the people—what did the young man want?

What was he singing about? He was singing about the crowd. About what they wanted. They wanted to be him: the center of attention. The logic of American mass events was embodied in the television installed above the young rock singer and his band, where the crowds' own faces were reflected back at them—the parable of the fifteen seconds of fame.

No Russian desired fame. A Russian desired death, and love. Fame was a curse.

But these were modern times; borders, always transitory, now barely existed. Colonel Stierlitz was comfortable with this. Inside his soul, he knew the truth of the oracular phoenix, to be reborn in the cold Siberian night, revivifed as Stalin was, the walking dead, rotted flesh made holy through the needs of the people and the land beneath their feet...

Colonel Stierlitz swayed to the music, his tie shining in the flashing blue lights, his hair slick, his hands warm on his lover's shoulder.

In bed that night he whispered things into Ekaterina's ear as he delved into her body, to look for something he had lost. Strange feelings overcame him at the moment of orgasm; a change of identity.

"I'm becoming American," he whispered in the dark, next to his mate, his mistress.

"You mustn't," Ekaterina said.

"I can feel it inside me. I want to play in a band."

"No, Maxy. Please."

"I feel I want it."

She rolled atop him, her delicious breasts pressed against his chest.

"I'll kill you if you play in a rock and roll band."

"Not rock and roll. Bluegrass. The music of the peasants."

"Hmmph."

"The banjo."

"You are insane." She glared down into his face.

"It is part of my mission."

"What do you mean?"

"The Swedish threat. They will not expect me to be playing the banjo. By throwing my enemy out of their comfort zone, I will gain control over them."

Ekaterina smiled.

"Fuck me again," she said.

The banjo was not easily learned. An African instrument at origin, it contained many rhythms that were foreign to Vsevolod's ear. His sucked on the hand-rolled cigarette stuck in his mouth as he tried to work out the transition in his fingers ...

There was something Russian about bluegrass. A peasant could understand it. It was the music of the land, not like rock and roll, which was the music of freedom. Bluegrass knew that the land devoured one; that it was hungry. It was music about death.

He played in the rehearsal studio he had rented with the Kremlin's money, to Stalin's outrage.

At last he stopped. He put the instrument into the locker and reset the combination and walked out onto the Long Beach street, sportcoat slung over his shoulder.

He knew now why so many Russians came to Los Angeles. It too was a city of death; a city of Angels. Those guardians of the afterlife.

Inside his body Colonel Stierlitz felt the small American child growing. The little being, homunculus—stepsister within.

He called his mistress to arrange dinner, then climbed on to the motorcycle he had rented and gunned the engine, cigarette still in his mouth. He spat it out onto the concrete as he turned a corner onto Second Street, right in front of a small, evil dog, barking insanely.

The logic of the internal combustion engine soothed Stierlitz's body; he ceased almost to think. Deep within, he assessed the intelligence he had gathered on the rock and roll star. The young man, named Francisco Smith, was twenty-five years old, worth twenty-five million dollars. He had a Swedish girlfriend. The girlfriend, whose name, improbably, was Junior Bunny, had been feeding Smith a designer drug cocktail Stockholm had developed exclusively for use by American rock stars. The servants of the Swedish king (their democracy was complete illusion) believed that drug dependence was the only route available to them to exert influence over the American body politic.

All of this was irrelevant to Stierltiz, however. He cared only about what the young man could do with his hands.

In a dream, shortly after landing at LAX, Colonel Stierlitz had seen the shaman in the forest who explained to him how certain hand motions propititated certain forest gods, known to the ancestors. Masonic hand-signals worked by the same method, Stierltiz reasoned; both a simple hand-sign designating that one belonged to the secret group, and a religious symbol capable of invokiong arcane energies from the aether.

The motions of the young man's hands over the rock and roll guitar were moving in Stierltiz's mind as he pulled the motorcyle over next to the Italian restaurant and went insdide. He took Ekterina's hand—she was beautiful, and in red, the most beautiful she would ever look, for she was pregnant now, two weeks—and they danced next to the band in dim light, the bar filled with Russian cigarette smoke.

He whispered in Ekaterina's ear: "My wife has woken up."

Ektaterina began to cry, silently, holding tight onto Stierltiz.

They moved to the beat of the music.

"I love you, Max," she said.

He watched her beautiful eyes.

"Do you love me?" she asked.

Max nodded.

In bed that night Max examined the phone he had stolen from the rock and roll star. Inside it was a picture of a beast, with black hair, standing under a red sky. It looked like a huge vole. Stierlitz shivered, and put the phone back in his briefcase.

Inside the banjo Max had concealed a small submachine gun. With it he would overturn the Swedish threat. Threats were all the coup were, he knew. Sweden, with or without her king, could never overpower the Russian steppe single-handedly. The Russians were a religious people; the Swedes atheists. Believers always triumphed.

On the flight back to Moscow, Max stroked the surface of his banjo. Ektaterina would remain behind, to have her child in America, so that he could be a dual-citizen. She would raise him there for nine months, then they would both reutrn to him in Moscow. The Russian state would pay for this. A cost he somewhat regretted. But he would repay the debt with blood.

4
Moscow

In his childhood, Stierlitz, who was not yet Stierlitz, had lived above a livery. The stench of the horses filled his bedroom, and he groomed them every day for Mr. Zapotnik, his employer.

The brown horse named Startail came to back to Stierlitz now, its strange face so like Stierlitz's own.

His mother was awake. So was most of Mother Russia. The Great Sleep had ended, and Red Square was filled with happy people stretching their legs. Comrade Stalin waved to them all from his dais, and a few waved back. Stierlitz saw the scene's great beauty and felt dread creep into his breast.

He reached for his banjo next to his bed and strummed the tune for "I've been working on the railroad."

"I've been working on the railroad, all the live long day," Stierlitz sang. "I've been working on the railroad, just to pass the time away."

His daughter was in his arms, awake. She embraced him, and then ran back outside in the sun to play.

Stierlitz picked up the telephone and called the bakery.

"You'll sell."

"What price?"

"I don't know. I'll be there in an hour. Make something nice for Stalin, won't you? It's his last night on Earth."

The baker hung up.

Stierlitz loaded the submachine gun and placed in its muzzle one of the white chrysanthemums his wife had placed in the vase by their bed.

5
Ekaterina

She took into the air, moving with her pregnancy now at seven months, flying in the air over Los Angeles, moving towards the Channel Islands, cold in her jumper, out, out over the Pacific, the peaceful ocean, seeking home:

Where is Vsevolod, she thought.

She stretched her arms out, watching the sun set over the ocean.

The raven flew near her.

"Kraaak" he said.

"Have you seen Max?" she asked.

"Kraak!"

The raven flew ahead, over the darkening Pacific.

Why would he leave me in America?

"Kraak!"

She tightened her sweater around her body.

The raven was flying high overhead.

Up ahead she could see a small ship with a light on its deck, in the mist.

She stepped onto the deck.

"Hello!" she said.

"Holy Jesus," said the sailor. "Come inside."

The raven was squawking at the window.

She felt disoriented.

"I need to sleep," she said.

"Not yet," said the sailor.

"What do you want?" she asked.

"Tell me what you are doing on my ship."

"I came a long way from Russia, following my husband. I am a minstrel. But I have lost my instrument. Where I am from, in Russia, we make instruments from bones."

"This is very interesting, but does not answer my question."

"I saw your light, and flew down."

"Well, we're too far from shore to take you back. Since you're a stowaway, consider yourself lucky I don't rape you and then throw you overboard. You can sleep here, in the galley. In the morning you'll cook us breakfast."

6
Moscow

Stierlitz held the transmitter in his hand; it showed Stalin's position. The good doctor had informed him the transmitter had been implanted in Stalin's neck, in this, his latest incarnation.

The transmitter indicated Stalin was below ground, slightly north of the Kremlin.

The waitress brought tea, and Stierlitz thanked her.

What had ever really known of Russia? The stories told to him as a child. The lessons, the schooling. None of it seemed pertinent now. His nation was someone else; someone he was only now meeting.

"You are Colonel Stierlitz?" asked the waitress. Stierlitz nodded. "A message for you," she said, handing him a paper.

On it, a crudely drawn scenario depicted the Pope, a man-wolf, and a large breasted woman fucking. Lines of blue ink scrawled across the torn page. It was signed, "Comrade Stalin."

Stierlitz sat in his canoe, moving under Moscow, in the canals. Moscow, which meant "marsh" in some ancient, pre-Slavic language. He rowed, flashlight strapped to his forehead with nylon.

The transmitter indicated Stalin was 600 meters away, to the northwest.

That Stalin remained alive was an abomination; why had Russia grown so fond of him? It was inexplicable to Stierlitz. The man needed to stay dead. More than most, even.

The Swedish threat was only a side effect of Stalin's meddling. To destroy Stalin permanently would take care of the external threats to Russia as well. But how to destroy him?

Stalin was five hundred meters distant now; the cursor blinked faster on Colonel Stierlitz's screen.

One can know many things in the dark; all the world lies within it. Stierlitz rowed deeper into the night beneath Moscow, listening to Stalin's cries. The insane zombie howled like a wolf, the brutal voice echoing off the ancient stone walls.

All the world lies within the dark because you can imagine many things in it. And it gets you to thinking: maybe the world you know in the light is just something someone dreamed up.

Samrkand had Alph, its sacred river, and Pluto had his Lethe and Styx; for Moscow it is the Volga, she whose waters unite most of Europe in her chemical embrace.

The oar in Stierlitz's hand was his whole world. His machine gun he kept in his lap.

He loved Russia, but more, he loved his land and its people, whatever their name. Why did they want this zombie alive? Still it confused him. The people of Moscow were confused; he knew that. He was confused too.

He would have to consult the shaman before this was through, but he hesitated to do so, fearing what might be the result.

He caught a glimpse of Stalin's leering face ahead, lit by a candle. He drew quickly and fired a burst of bullets towards the creature. Stalin ducked away.

Stierlitz rowed faster.

Now that his family was awake it was important for Moscow to be strong for them; for all the recently awoken. All of Europe had been asleep, for a long time. Being in Long Beach had taught Stierltiz this. The sound of the banjo, like the sound of an African drum, stirred something in him. Some ancient ancestor moved inside his bowels and his blood, insisting that things be put right.

But if he killed Stalin and the man stayed dead ... what then?

Who would Moscow be then.

To awake a sleeping giant, the people of the countryside and their cities ... it was an enormous thing. Like watching an asteroid approach. Like watching the earth open, its terible maw steaming below one ...

What did the land need? What did it require?

His service. And it would have it. But how could he know what services it needed the most?

Too many questions, even for a spy.

He reloaded his magazine, slipping the bullets in by feel.

7
Ekaterina

The nearness of the ocean lent Ekaterina's mind the feeling of being not-quite-there, a charming half-life, while she cooked the eggs and bacon over the small gas stove in the galley.

Her baby enjoyed the smell of it; awaking as the bacon cooked, and kicking her.

Inside her was the ocean, and below her.

"Good work on the bacon," said the sailor.

She looked at him, and his beard. She put more bacon on the grill.

Outside, clouds blew over the ship. She began to sing in a low voice, and her baby listened, smelling the bacon. Hearing the Russian sounds in her throat.

She ate one of the strips, with the sailor watching.

8
Beneath Moscow

Underneath Moscow, where the light limns low, in grinning faces, and spectral wails, in the mid-stream rant and row ... row in, Stierlitz:

Row into the undertow.

"I must be a crazy person," Stierlitz mutters. And he is. But so are we. Aren't you, Stierlitz?

"Stalin!" he shouts. But just more laughter answers, in the distance. And the rats.

The transmitter is malfunctioning. Stalin seems to be right over him. He hears a sound in the rock above his head. He raises his gun—

Stalin drops on top of him, the boat capsizes into the dark water, and they sink below, embracing one another. Stalin grinning, with his brown teeth.

Stierlitzs knees the zombie in the groin to no effect, jams his elbow into Stalin's ear, to same. Stalin makes to bite Stierlitz's neck and Stierltiz twists free, in horror, to the surface:

His transmitter blinks red by the side of the canal, casting crazy laser shadows.

He pulls himself out of the freezing water. Looks back down. No sign of Stalin. But the transmitter says he is still near.

Stierlitz takes one of the emergency torches from the wall of the cavern, put there in the event of sudden nuclear attack by Americans, and cracks it in half to activate the chemicals. He lights it, sputtering red sparks, and holds it close over the dark water.

Stalin looks up, his eyes amused, one fathom below the surface. Stierlitz screams down at the undead czar. Stalin smiles, and swims away.

Stierlitz follows, with the transmitter and torch, his teeth chattering.

Muginn alights on his shoulder.

"Odin," says Muginn.

Stierlitz turns west, moving into the region below the Moscow suburbs. Muginn flutters on his shoulder.

Muginn whispers in his ear, of Ektaterina.

Tears wet Stierlitz's eyes, and he strokes Muginn's head, who flies off. Stierlitz finds an access ladder to a hatch, and goes back above into freezing Moscow rain.

"Ekaterina is freezing!" chattered Stierlitz, huddled in his bed, his wife watching him with skeptical eyes as she sipped her tea.

"Drink your tea," she said.

Stierlitz sipped it and slipped back into his fever.

Mrs. Stierlitz went to call Denisovich.

"It is a grave case," said Denisovich.

"What is to be done, doctor?" said Mrs. Stierlitiz.

"I will have to call the spirit shaman, The Worker."

"Then do it."

Denisovich built the traditional fire on the roof of Max's house, the smoke signal waving from the carpet.

In the distance in the trees, The Worker saw the smoke.

He climbed down from the tree where he had been sleeping. It had been a nice rest with most of Moscow asleep. But now they were waking up.

He moved like a Russian bear, though he was tall and skinny, lumbering through the forest at the edge of Moscow, into the suburbs, where the old ladies brought him out crepes to eat, hot from the pan, when they saw him, curtsying politely, moving, always moving, over the many steppes of Asia, and the many steps of consciousness, into the drum at the heart of the heart of the sun ...

The Worker knew many things, which, he would argue, was just another way of saying that he knew nothing, a prisoner of forces too large for him to understand—in other words, a free man.

His ancestors had used smoke signals and so did he. If he chose to sleep in the woods, what of that? Was he not as civilzied as any a Russian? Did he not dream in the night, of bears? And circuses? Was his smile not wide, and deadly?

Even the stranniks feared The Worker. Even the priests.

It is so dangerous to be feared.

When people fear you, you must be so careful.

If you are not, you might be murdered.

The Worker knocked on Max's door by Red Square. Denisovich answered.

"Thank you for coming, Mr. Worker."

"You're welcome," said the Worker, smiling. "Is tea prepared?"

"Yes, come in."

The Worker sat in the sitting room, drinking the mountain tea.

"Moscow has changed," said The Worker.

"Yes," said Denisovich.

"I am worried," said The Worker.

"Don't be," said Denisocvich. "These things come and go."

"If you say so," said The Worker. "Where is your patient?"

"Right this way."

Denisovich led him into Max's bedroom where Mrs. Stierltiz was tending him and The Worker began to sing, as the Navajo too sing, as all our ancetors sang to sickness, to see what kind of sickness it might be. One has to communciate, you see. One must listen. And then speak.

He sang for many hours, as Moscow grew dark. And Max dreamed terrible dreams, there in the dark.

9
Abomination

In the Middle Ages priests reasoned, falsely, that the root of the word "abomination" must be "ad hominem" — against man. But it actually comes from an older root, "bad omen."

So the abomination is not some antichrist, some ultimate evil, but rather worse, in some ways: it is a signal of bad things to come. A sign that things are turning sour. The ill wind. And the fake smile. The toppling tower, and the burning downs, and the shower, of blood ...

Stalin grew in the night. He grew in the night beneath his city. In the marshland. In the dark water. Stalin grew like a reed, sucking it up. For even as canon, and cannon, come from reed, the simple cylinder, and canon wars amongst priests are the simple question: which documents can we afford to save? Which shall we take with us?

So Stalin is a canon, a reed, a vessel, sucking up, the information, the qualities, the mysteries, of his city, and his water, city named for marsh, in a land named by Vikings, for their oars, in a region ruled by shamans ...

The shaman is the worker. Working to do, and to be, to creep into the right places, for the right orders—whatever you can! Whatever you can manage.

Max is waking.

We are waking, Max.

Max, are you awake!

"I am."

Stalin is growing, Max.

"It is only a bad dream."

You are awake, Max!

"Denisovich! Bring me my medicine!"

But he is alone in his house. His wife, his daughter, gone.

In an empty Moscow.

A mausoleum.

The Worker stood by his bed, humming.

"Worker," said Max. "Thank God you're here. I'm having a bad dream. Wake me up."

But The Worker just kept humming, swaying gently back and forth by Max's bed.

"Worker!"

Max got out of bed, and wrapped his robe around him.

Outside in Red Square, Stalin's head had emerged from the plaza stones, like a huge ripe orange. Or a strange mushroom. The evil thing smiled a beatific smile.

The Worker kept humming.

"Worker," Max whispered. The Worker opened one eye.

"Worker, it's Stalin. He's huge."

The Worker closed his eye again.

Stalin screamed outside, a sound heard only in dreams. And things like dreams.

As one does in dreams, Max went outside in his

robe.

"You're too big, Stalin," said Max to the enormous head. "You're enormous."

"Yes," said Stalin. "Go get a pavement saw, won't you, I'm stuck."

"This has to stop, Stalin. The Motherland can't bear you any more. I can't either. I'm going to kill you again. This time, Comrade, you must stay dead."

"Just get the pavement saw, I said."

Max went to get the explosives. He turned east, down towards the barracks. The Worker stepped up behind him, following.

"Not this way, Max. Blowing him up won't be enough."

"I know. But what then?"

"I don't know. I'm not smart enough for this."

"We just have to blow him up, and pray."

"I'm going back into the woods."

"Oh, keep me company won't you, anyway? We're the only ones in Moscow."

The Worker hummed for a bit, as they walked toward the barracks in the Moscow night.

"You know, Max, now that I think of it, blowing him up may work after all."

"Thank you for your vote of confidence."

"He is abomination. But if we destroy him, there will be worse to follow."

"We will bear it."

"I hope so."

The two men strapped the C4 all around Stalin's screaming head, wearing earmufs The Worker kindly provided, to shield them from the horrible demon's noise.

Then they blew up the huge evil head.

The sun was coming up.

Max got back into bed with his beautiful wife, and made a quick phone call to sanitary services, to clean up the mess.

10
The Pacific

Stalin's ghost flew through the sky, passing over the Pacfic, where Ekaterina stood at the prow of the dirty fishing trawler, a living mermaid bust, holding her pregnant belly. And he passed into space above.

Ekterina watched the sun rise and knew she was in trouble. Why had she taken up with a married man? It would be a life of hardship for her and her child. And why had she left America then? For love? Stupid.

She went to the captain.

"I quit," she said. "Throw me overboard."

"We can't throw pregnant women overboard," he said. "At least have your child first, then you can jump."

"I won't do it," she said. "You must throw me over now."

"Don't be silly. Have a drink."

"I can't drink, I'm pregnant," she said.

"Tea then," said the captain.

They drank together in silence.

The captain had a large beard.

"I like your beard," she said.

"I like yours too," he said.

She laughed.

11
Moscow

Vsevolod played his banjo. In midst of his playing, his wife began to cry. His daughter put her
hand on her mother's shoulder, watching her father.

Part 2
Flight

Colonel Stierlitz was approaching Berlin. The city was veiled in smoke from the fires. "Must have forgotten to turn off my iron," Stierlitz thought with slight irritation.

-- traditional Russian joke

12
Moscow

Who knows which Russia it is, the one that burned down, or the one that rose from the ashes? Which life is it we are leading? Waking, sleeping, in between, dreams and reality and both, inter-mixing, the sky and the sea—

Stierlitz, tell us, have you been much over this Earth of ours, with your spying and missions and marches, your many caviar dinners and lattes late at night, vodka and vodka, which means "little water," a little water, eh Stierlitz?

"Yes, a little water."

He drank.

Stierlitz, let me be the microphone. I want to

be microphone again.

"You're a very good microphone."

Thank you so much, Stierltiz. Am I really?

"Yes."

Stierlitz, what can we do? You must save Russia.

"I'll figure it out."

Play the banjo again, Stierlitz.

"I've already finished."

The sun has risen. Moscow is awake. The Americans are afraid. Ekaterina sails west. Stalin is dead.

Stierlitz walks down to his cafe.

"Soldier! I haven't seen you for a while!"

The soldier ignores him.

"Solder! Hey there!"

He looks back once, at Stierlitz. Then he keeps walking.

Stierlitz was disturbed. "The man must be having love problems," he thought.

He opened the door to his cafe only to find the owner staring him in the face.

"I can't have you here Stierlitz," he said.

"What?"

"The Intelligence Services aren't welcome here any more."

"What do you mean?"

"You must go."

"But I live here."

"This is my cafe and you must go!"

"Well damn you to hell!"

Stierlitz walked off. He went to his bar.

The door to his bar was boarded up. He pounded his fist on the wood.

In disgust he queued outside the government liquor shop for a dram of vodka, which he drank in the street, like a musician.

Where had his Moscow gone?

Would he ever find out?

"God damn this city!" he shouted. People ignored him, except for an old drunk by the train station, who flipped him off.

He found himself again my Red Square, observing the re-paving of the stones, cleaning up after Stalin's final death.

Lenin's grave had been moved too; it was a garden now. He sat on a bench there, watching the people. The sky was beautiful.

"This is not my Moscow," he muttered.

The little girl he had met in the square before came up to him.

"Colonel Stierlitz," she said.

"Mademoiselle."

"Are you well, Colonel?"

"No." He crossed his arms.

"What is the matter?" She sat down next to him.

The Colonel said nothing.

"What is it?" she asked.

"I'm lonely," he said.

She nodded.

"I'm lonely for a Moscow I have never seen," he said.

"Me too," she said.

13
The Pacific

Coming home is a long way away. Ekaterina, daughter of Russian tortures, whose name was the daughter of yet older Armenian tortures, whose body was subject to the motions of the Earth, whose face greeted the dawn, whose belly bore a son for Vsevolod Vladimirovich Vladimirov, watched the water move under the trawler.

The sailor was saying something to her, shouting something, behind her.

But the ocean was louder, the sea—the sea within her:

She turned to look at the sailor. His face so like a boy.

Still she could not hear him; she walked over to him.

"What?"

"You look beautiful standing there."

"I'm a married woman," she said.

"I don't think you are," he said.

She went back into the galley to make lunch.

The Vikings founded Russia. 'Rus' means 'row.' And so, the history of Russia can be understood as a history of ships.

Where was the first sea vessel?

Was it Madagascar?

Not long after the asteroid that made the Gulf of Mexico and killed the dinosaurs, the lemurs, beset with an urgent energy, 60 million yeas behind us now, their bodies moved urgently onto the kelp, to sea, to sea, to sea, and east: into Madagascar.

But what other creatures, what others, before them, also made their journeys, over the water.

Even the Face of God, hovering over them, our own face, looking down: at what lies beneath, our soul:

Ekaterina kissed the sailor in the dark.

14
Canals

Stierlitz returned to the basement marsh—the sewers and the canals beneath Moscow.

The musician was there—his friend.

"I am back," said Stierlitz.

"I fear for you, brother," said the musician.

They walked through the torchlight underneath Moscow.

"Stalin may return, but he will not be Stalin," said the musician.

"Some other evil who threatens Russia," muttered Stierlitz.

"It may even be you," said the musician.

"I would sooner kill myself than harm my country," said Stierlitz.

"I know, Colonel. But these times are strange. I myself wonder, who it is I'm becoming now."

"I too. Sometimes, I admit, I have thought of returning to America. I learned to play the banjo there."

"Ha ha ha! Play me something then!"

Stierlitz played, standing next to the canal, the bluegrass of Appalachia improbably transported under the steppe, in the marsh basin, under the city of his Viking and forest peasant ancestors, enriching some spark whose breath even Stierlitz, with his keen eyesight, could not see, only music:

Whose other name is there. After music.

We must pause for a time, to let them play.

My grandfather also played the banjo.

"But this story is about me, microphone. Tell your grandfather's story another time."

My grandfather was born in Brooklyn. He fled the Great Depression, to Los Angeles. How he learned to play the banjo, I haven't learned. He did not call it Dixieland, what he played. He called it "funny music."

"Microphone, you are American?"

Yes, Stierlitz.

"There is something I do not understand then. How was it that you came to interrogate me in the apartment building in Moscow, after I woke up?"

I don't know, Stierltiz. You must tell me, if you wish. I'm not sure I can figure it out. But first, play your banjo. I have a feeling it's going to be very important.

I caught an evening cry
Under the sun
No Daddy for me
Not no more
I got rhythm
And I got reason
But I don't have the sun!

15
Sea

The sea is its own teacher. Mohammed, the sailor, grew terrible burned well great and manly but not ever —not ever done— whose name we might utter (our own) and his, and hers, Ekaterina.

Ekaterina, whose summer, not yet fading, whose elegance, now at its height, whose rightenousness—well, I don't know about her righteousness.

They fucked. Over the sea.

Moving west.

Now — bearing the bitter truth is my task, and I have found it to be sweet. But Stierlitz, you whose majesty is our own, over our nightmares, and over our campfires, our hero, only watching us, little man, with a moustache, and a fever, for your own truth, what can I tell you?

Your appetites, Stierlitz, reap their own rewards, and our future, tied to yours, must tell us what we would like to hear (and also what we fear) and also just what is to happen:

Ekaterina cried out in the night.

The dignity of some delirious affair—especially one whose fruits are not a threat to dominant patriarchies (she can't get pregnant when she's pregnant!)—what is the fruit of that dignity? The fruit of a king's dignity can be an empire. The fruit of a child's, a star. Or a road. We can't deny it its essence. All affairs—sexual and otherwise—are completely their own, incorruptible, unavoidable, carrying with them all that they are and will become having erupted against us, joined in us.

Stierlitz had abandoned her. But she would take him back.

Over the vessel the crow flew. Watching.

Mohammed, who came from a sailing family of some thousand generations, considered for the first time—and quite seriously—leaving the sea. To follow this woman, into Russia. Into a country who despised him and his religion.

Madness, of course. A brown man, a Muslim, following a beautiful young Russian woman into Moscow?

One might as well shoot oneself first and get it over with, right?

We'll see.

16
Moscow

Who shall know the beginning and the end?
Am I to know?
How can I know?
How would I ever know which to put at the end?
Stierlitz, tell me.
"Shh, I'm playing."
Stierlitz, tell me. Tell, won't you?
"Shhh."
Stierlitz is going to America. Going to America.
Going to America.

Going to America!
America!
America!
America!
Stierlitz, aren't you?
"Shut up, I said!"
He's crying. The Russian is crying.
No one may know why. No one will know why.
Stierlitz, I love you.
"I'm going to kill you, you fucking microphone."
Stierlitz! Go to America!
In America, tell me: who are we?
"I am Vsevolod Vladimirovich Vladimirov. If I
am truly to depart the motherland, on a long mis-
sion, I must have a good story."
Stierlitz picks up his telephone.
"Semyonov. I want to be reassigned. To Amer-

ica."

"America, Stierlitz? What's come over you?"

"Send me, boss. Please."

"We need you here, Stierlitz!"

"Boss. Please."

"I'll give you six months Stierlitz. All right? But then you're coming back."

"Thanks boss."

Stierlitz hung up his phone and embraced his friend the musician in the twilight of the canals beneath Moscow. Together they rowed back out into the Russian daylight.

The daylight moved over Stierlitz as he climbed the steps to his apartment, and embraced his wife. They made love on the floor of his entry room. And when he was finished he put back on his coat, and walked back down the stairs, and got into a cab.

"To the airport," he said.

17
Ocean

Stierlitz?
"Hmmm."
Tell me, Stierlitz.
"Hmm."
I love you, Stierlitz.
"Shhhh."

And Stierlitz thinks:
No America, no America for me, I am unworthy
of it.
I am Russian.
I am Old world.
I am ... lost.
I am a servant.
Not a master.
But I am, perhaps, even a nobleman.
Going to the land with no nobility.
Where does it stop?
This absence in my brain
I need a drink
"Waiter!"
What is it sir.
"Vodka on the rocks!"
That'll be ten dollars sir.
"Goddamned Russian patriotism. It will be end
of us. Down with the world beneath the world.

Down with the czar! Down with the ..."

Not the Kremlin, Stierlitz?

"No, no. It will stand. It will stand! I've had enough of it though! I've had enough of that god-damned mushroom! I will be free, if it kills me. I will be free. I will be free."

18
The Old Woman

The bitter liquid drips through her palms, the woman in the hovel underground.

This liquid is a poison, and a powerful hallucinogen, made out of bark, and water.

She is almost immune to it, having made it for many years.

In the north country where the sun flees, the soul has a memory that is not entirely its own; that there were others here, before us, and indeed, contemporary with us, ghosts, or norns, spirits, beings close by and unseen; it is bitter.

But bitterness can be sweet, at the right time. In the right mouth.

19
Stierlitz Dances

Stierlitz is dancing, in a dark room. No one can see him but me.

He makes his pirhouettes. Jeter, pliet, down, up.

The walls are luminous in darkness, like home.

The spy is home, inside the dark, dancing, moving to the rhythm of his heart.

Someone is knocking on the door to the studio.

"Who is it?" cried Stierlitz.

"Max, it's me!" says Ekaterina.

Stierltiz opens the door.

She has been crying.

"You son of a dog! You left me in America!"

"Where am I now?" asks Stierlitz.

She looks around; suddenly she is confused too. She looks beautiful.

"What did you do Maxy!"

"I don't know. I was playing the banjo ..."

"That god damned instrument!"

"Then I was dancing."

"You abandoned me."

"No, I didn't!"

In the dark room of dreams all is available for inquiry, and all is masked. For the masquerade. Dance with me, and I will show you Colonel Stierlitz, come what may, in his last altruistic adventure, before his great season came to an end, and other patriots moved their way forward, into the breach ...

Would that we could all be Stierlitz, eh? Wedded to the peat and the rich ruin of this earth, wedded to the soil. And yet ... so we are. Stierlitz merely believes better than most. He knows on which side his bread is buttered.

20
Stierlitz Arrives in Koreatown

This place is strange, he thinks. *Not at all like Long Beach.*

He strums his banjo to feel the heft of it in his hands and the heft of the sound of the instrument in the space around the Wiltern theater.

Above him pigeons fly around the blue-green hotel-turned-music-hall, following the sounds of Stierlitz's instrument.

Another Russian, one of them thinks.

At least he has an instrument, thinks another.

Stierltiz plays until it gets dark, and the homeless people begin to make fun of him.

Taking him for a busker who forgot to put down his hat, one old Korean lady begrudgingly inserts a worn dollar into the pocket of Stierlitz's jeans.

Stierlitz sings the blues into the night.

In his apartment, his phone is ringing.

"Semyonov here. Stierlitz, how are you liking your new digs?"

"They are very adequate. The light is beautiful here."

"Don't enjoy it too much, Max. You won't be staying long."

"I know. What is the news?"

"The Swedish King's coup attempt failed, as you

know. The Vikings may have conquered us 2,000 years ago but they won't be doing it again any time soon. What is interesting to us now is why they attempted it at all. Are they merely a pawn of the Americans? Is it a feint for some other maneuver?

"Ania Bolotnikova I have assigned to assist you. Be careful, Max. Long Beach isn't what it used to be."

"What do you mean, boss?"

"Just be careful. Find out what the Swedes were up to. Their embassy in Los Angeles is also expecting you. Arrive tomorrow. And Max, your girlfriend. Did you know she's in Moscow?"

"I have to go, Yulian. Pray for me."

"Getting religious, Max?"

"Always."

He hung up.

He held the banjo in his arms, like a woman.

The guide of the Museum of the October Revolution demonstrates to visitors the skeleton of the Civil War hero V.I.Chapaev.

-And what is that small skeleton behind him?

-That is V.I.Chapaev in childhood, explains the guide.
- traditional Russian joke

21
Moscow

Ekaterina was getting drunk. She had left her Muslim lover in Glebovskoye Podvorye, the old Jewish ghetto, feeling a bit bad about it, but she wanted to be alone.

Now she drank, feeling the liquor against her throat, watching the light outside the bar turn from white to blue.

"One should not drink when pregnant," observed the bartender.

"Give me another," she said.

He poured.

"I flew over the Pacific," Ekaterina said.

"Good for you," said the bartender.

The light was getting bluer and bluer as dusk approached. Through the misted window the light was like milk.

"My husband has left me," Ekaterina said.

"Good riddance to him."

"I wish he were dead!" She slammed down the shot glass.

The bartender nodded.

"He never did anything for me. I did everything for him!"

"More vodka?" asked the bartender.

Ekaterina nodded.

"I'm going to kill him. He will suffer!"

"No need to kill him. He suffers enough, without you."

Ekaterina laughed. "He doesn't suffer enough."

Glebovskoye Podvorye had changed significantly since its days in tsarist Russia, when it had been a nightmarish city-within-a-city, part Jewish market, part Jewish prison. Now it served the one remaining launch facility in Russia, following Baikonur's decommissioning. The Jewish community, once largely decrepit and in rags, was now one of the best-off in Moscow, and they paid slightly higher taxes because of it, partly in kind: they maintained the launch facility with their own hands. They were also some of the only Muscovites who would hire Muslims.

The little girl in Red Square watched the launch with a thrill in her heart. In space, she knew, Russians were free.

22
Mohammed

Mohammed labored on the blast zone, polishing its white ceramic tiles.

Axel approached him, wearing a Russian hat.

"You are Mohammed?" Axel said.

"What do you want?" Mohammed asked, mopping the blast zone in Glebovskoye Podvorye.

"I want to go into space," Axel said.

"The next tourist launch is in three weeks; you'll have to sign up and pay in the office." He gestured with his hand.

"No, I want to go into space with you."

Mohammed stood, holding his mop. "Who are you?"

"My name is Axel. I am with the Vikings."

"The Vikings, who are they?"

"You know, The Vikings."

"I have work to do." He went back to mopping.

"It will be worth it to you." Axel showed him an envelope, bursting with American C-notes.

"I can do nothing. Even if you paid me. Go ask someone else."

"I'll be back. And when I am, we're going into space."

Mohammed shook his head.

Axel stood atop one of the observation decks, observing the launch facility. An old Jewish babushka, blue-grey headscarf stretched over her grey head, said:

"It's a messy place, isn't it."

"Yes," said Axel.

"Something tell me you're planning to make even a bigger mess. One I'll have to clean up."

"No, nothing like that, grandmother," said Axel.

"I don't believe you." Suddenly the old woman had a knife at the Viking's neck. "What do you want?" she asked.

23
Speaking to Stierlitz

You're dancing, Stierlitz!
"Get me out of here."
Not until you tell me what you mean.
"What do you want to hear, torturer?"
Tell me the truth, Stierlitz. Why did you come?
"To save the motherland."
How will you do it, Stierlitz?
"I'll die if I have to."

24
Long Beach

Stierlitz followed the man through the parking garage, watching his hat bob amdist the cars.

He's like a fishing boat, thought Stierlitz.

The man was likely armed; he had to be careful. No sense getting killed over this; not when his wife and now too his mistress were awaiting him at home. He'd just needed a break. Did he regret it now? Too late for that.

The man turned and fired and Stierlitz felt his life shoot through his veins, a thrilling sensation. He dropped to the ground but the bullet had already missed him.

"*Chyort voz'mi!*" whispered Stierlitz, watching for the hatted man, and crawling to the left, towards the elevators.

"Colonel Stierlitz!" called out the man with the hat.

"Yes? What is it!" cried out Stierltiz. He sounded like a schoolmarm to his own ears.

"I have a message for you. Get the fuck out of Long Beach."

The man appeared then, a huge beard like a strannik, black on his face, and a small snub-nosed gun pointed right at Stierlitz. He fired then, missing, striking the concrete by Stierlitz's head. Stierlitz stared.

"Today, Stierlitz," said the man, smiling. Then

he put the gun back in his pocket and walked off.

We must preserve the dignity of our hero and so will not mention the unfortunate occurance which led Stierlitz to seek the bathroom. After a few minutes he emerged again, and called his boss.

"Someone wants to kill me, boss," he said. But there was no one on the other end of the phone.

Was he losing his touch? What had Semyonov said? Ania Bolotnikova was to meet him. But she hadn't called. He'd received a message instead, to meet a contact in downtown Long Beach. He'd been played like a rookie.

He found the security guard at the parking garage entrance.

"Excuse me, did you just see a bearded man with a hat walk out of here?"

"Yeah, a few minutes ago," the guard said, smiling.

"Is something funny?" Stierlitz said, smiling awkwardly.

"Yeah, he told me to give you a message. He said a guy with a Russian accent would be looking for him. He said to meet him at the Red Room."

"I see. Thank you. Where is this Red Room please."

"Right down there," the guard pointed, and indeed, standing outside the bar was a beautiful woman in a red dress, serving as barker.

Stierlitz bowed slightly to the guard and went back onto the street.

He decided to call his wife. But she was not answering her phone either.

"Is all of Moscow asleep again?" Stierltiz muttered, walking towards the bar.

The beautiful barker in the red dress did her work on the sidewalk, and Siterlitz realized after a moment she was speaking the lyrics of David Bowie's "Changes":

"Still don't know what I was waiitng for. And my time was running wild. A million dead-end streets. Every time I thought I'd got it made. It seemed the taste was not so sweet ..."

Where Bowie's words had been lament, the barker's were hortatory, enticing one, to the dead end streets within:

"Your ticket," said the woman, as Stierlitz reached the door.

Stierlitz took the ticket and stared at her a moment. He went inside.

The Red Room lived up to its name—all dim red lighting and black leather seats.

"Vodka please," Stierlitz told the bartender. He eyed the clientele. The bearded man was nowhere to be seen.

25
Speaking to Stierlitz

Tell me, great century, is it right that Stierlitz should have been the one to do it, the one to set off the nuclear doomsday weapon, long after the probability of such an occurance was close to zero?

What of the logic of it. What of the disaster.

But all of this is not yet.

Not yet.

Colonel Stierlitz's Motherland is not yet, perhaps—it is a land yet to be.

Is his Motherland close to us? Is it one we might know to?

Tell us, Stierlitz!

"I cannot speak. This, this is too terrible."

You must speak, Stierlitz. I am your torturer.

"What do you want me to say?"

Your Motherland, Stierltiz, where is it?

"I thought it was in Russia."

No longer.

"Where is it then?"

In space.

"I don't want to go into space."

You're already there, Stierlitz.

26
The Boy

Moscow is black.

The great black Moscow looms like a dog—a wolf—over the night. The rich rewards of night: what a mercy it is. What a mercy, darkness, in Moscow, like a flood, after a drought, the dark, making everything clean, mysterious, at one with the cosmos. In the dark, as Shel Silverstein knew, we are all one, the same people, moving towards our shared goal ...

Luminouis unreal Colonel Stierlitz opens his book and reads in the darkness of Moscow (this is five years ago, before the events so far related), and he is reading, the story of a young boy.

In the darkness Stierlitz can almost see him, hovering in the darkness, his pale face a moon, his eyes, terrible to behold, that sadness in that young face, like the eyes of a Druid, beholding the end of his tree.

Stierlitz cries out to him, in the dark, throwing the book down onto the cobblestones but the boy is in the book, and the boy is on the street.

"What does this mean?" Stierlitz asked himself.

He told his wife; she told him it was a ghost, and that they should pray, and ignore it.

Now in Los Angeles Stierlitz has seen the boy.

The boy is Korean, he realizes. A young Korean boy. In Koreatown.

Stierlitz smokes a cigarette on his balcony. Somewhere, the boy is looking at him.

27
Los Angeles

"What did you think you were doing, Stierlitz, when you came to LA?"

"I wanted to get out of Moscow," Stierlitz told the bearded man, in the LA club.

Above them the stars are shining; tinsel.

"I wanted to get out of Moscow and so I did. What did you think were you doing, when you came to LA?"

"I was following a woman," the bearded man said. "She left me."

Stierlitz nodded.

"Later I met another woman. She got me in to the business I'm in now."

"What business is that?" asked Stierlitz.

"The same one you're in, Stierlitz."

The singer got up onto the stage, the woman who had been the barker.

If I ever been seen
I been seen by you.
If I ever been in the dark,
I been in it by you.

If I never seen
The way you moved ...

If I never seen—

"I love this city," said Stierlitz.

"But it's not your city," said the bearded man.

"No, it isn't."

"We need you to do something for us, Stierlitz."

"What's that?"

"Moscow has something that we want. A dome."

"What?"

"The southeast dome of the Kremlin. LA wants it. For a festival. We want to rent it."

Stierlitz cracked a faint smile.

"You want to rent a dome of the Kremlin?"

"That's right."

"Who is you?"

"A consortium of interested parties in Los Angeles."

"Even if I could arrange such a thing, which obviously no one could, why would I ever do it?"

"Because we have something that you want, Stierlitz."

"I want only to serve the Motherland."

"We have your motherland in a box."

Something came over Stierlitz; a memory.

"I have it right here with me." The man took out a shoebox and opened it. It was filled with dirt; Stiertliz could smell the Moscow soil.

"Sir, what is it that you think ..."

But the smell of it, Stierlitz knew: this was ... there was no word for it. A spell, if you like. A signal from some horrifying dark ...

"Get us the dome. For a month. And we will return the soil to you and your city."

Stierlitz got up and left the bar, feeling nauseous. The city loomed over him, oppressive. He called a cab and rode in the back to his street on Western Avenue and climbed the stairs to his apartment and looked out of the window. He thought, for the first time in a very long while, about jumping.

The noise of the city soothed him a bit; it reminded him of home.

He picked up his phone and called the musician in Moscow.

"I need you to get on a plane," he said. "Tomorrow."

28
Koreatown

It's Koreatown, Jack ...

Stierlitz hovered outside the apartment building where he had seen the queen go in. In Moscow one could loiter for hours and never attract a
moment's attention; here in LA half a second was
long enough. You could not stop moving.

Stierlitz is running. Down the alleyway.
Who knows the secret?
Of the dark times ahead.
Which sirens know the secret.
Calling us into the secret, in the dark ...
Stierlitz?
I feel I want to scream, Stierltiz thought.
Stierlitz, don't scream yet.
"AAAAAAAAAAAAAAAAAAAAAAAAAAAAH!"
The blank bright alleyway now warm, from his
honest startled voice, brought Stierlitz back to
earth, chasing the queen. Finally he cornered her,
the drag queen, in the Koreatown alley.

"You were the one I saw in my dream. The
horse. On the Russian steppe."

"I don't know what you're talking about man! I
have a knife, and I know how to use it!"

Stierlitz raised his hands. "I'm sorry I scared
you. I only want to hire you, as a singer. It's very

important. That's all. I'm leaving you my card." He placed it carefully on the asphalt, a peace offering.

"You got to do something for me, man. You're a killer, aren't you?"

Stierlitz nodded, slowly.

"I got someone. Someone real bad. He's a Hollywood man. He's in my house. He's up there now. If I go back up there … he's gonna try to kill me. He says I owe him money."

Stierlitz nodded. Inside, he felt something click into place.

"This man is gonna try to kill me. You want me to sing, you got to help me out. Help me get out of this! I need a bad dude like you."

"Okay," said Stierlitz. "Go up to your apartment. I will follow."

Though these be dark times the light she follows at a discreet distance, wondering, when it will be, the time, for our embrace of her, so quietly, if only for a moment, the secret tryst, of love, for her, in our shadows, turning, towards the muse, of our night, turning, Stierlitz, in your love, for your country, and your people:

Stierlitz drives the knife into the man's body, listening to the sound of his bones accept the metal. He takes it out and drives it in again.

All around him he can feel the forces coalescing; what he had feared, for so many years, ever since he had seen the boy's face.

Outside the Moscow musician plays and Stierlitz climbs into the horsedrawn carriage with the queen headed for Hollywood for an important performance.

In our darkness we worship the light.

29
Hollywood

The bad man is dead (worse than Stierlitz? Yes, we can say that ...) and Stierlitz flees through the night, accompanying the man wearing women's clothes into Hollywood.

She slips the driver an extra note and he urges the horses forward faster; traffic neighs about them—the horses are impervious.

The centrality of the dream is the secret to Hollywood—no longer just American—and so all cultures and their dreams can find shelter here, under our palm trees ...

The musician plays on Hollywood and Vine, busking, and Stierlitz follows the drag queen down the subway stairs into a side tunnel where she shows him a glimmering photograph.

"It's my child," the drag queen says. The photograph looks simultanously fresh and old; a reprint of some 70s chemical developer.

It is the boy.

"That's your son?"

"Yes!"

"Where is he now?"

"He lives down here."

"In the subway?"

"Yes!"

"What do you need me to do?"

"I want you to talk to him. He won't listen to

me! Tell him to come out of here, this is no place for a boy!"

"But how old is he now?"

"Eighteen."

"How do I find him?"

The drag queen, Shaundra, turns and calls down the passageway:

"Johnny!"

A scrawny young man peers around the corner.

"Hey," the young man says.

"Hello," says Stierlitz.

"Got a smoke?" says Johnny.

Stierlitz hands him one. The boy lights it and sucks in the smoke, exhaling, watching Stierlitz.

"I'll leave you men alone," says Shaundra, fluttering. "I'll be back!"

Stierlitz lights a cigarette too. They smoke in silence.

"You're Russian."

"Yes."

"How do you know my mother?"

"A friend of a friend."

"I'm not leaving the subways."

Stierlitz nodded.

"You can't make me."

"Nor do I wish to."

"Mom doesn't understand how it is down here now. It's good. We've got everything we need. Electricity, everything! I don't need to go back up there."

"Your mother must miss you."

"She sees me all the time! She's just paranoid. She's always paranoid."

"Perhaps she has reason to be."

"What do you want, man?"

"I want to understand."

30
Hell of light

Stierlitz came into it, watching the light of the subway play over his legs. It occured to him that this was how it had been, long ago, and was so now, he, and the place, intertwined.

He and the place moving: reacting and twisting into this hell of light.

How naive of us to imagine we can examine and play with these stories of ghosts and goblins and religions without accepting them back into the universe we inhabit, without paying our toll, a toll whose amount is unquantifiable, and whose time of payment is forever.

Of course, we are not the same. Nor is Stierlitz.

He cries out, on the subway. He screams. A black man hears him, and shouts back. No one else does.

The city moves over him; it listens to him. Suddenly Colonel Stierlitz is of interest to Los Angeles, when he never was before.

The light moves him; shining paths, horrible destinies, worlds and worlds within worlds, screaming.

The city is falling around him; the city is climbing around him.

He emerges from the Koreatown subway surrounded with light; drowning in it.

The light moves in waves over his face, through

his hair, through his skin, through his organs, changing every particle of him, changing everything.

Everything he was is different now. Almost he should have a new name, but I am afraid to give him one, so he will still be Colonel Stierlitz. Now subtly altered.

Now Stierlitz has arrived at the grave site of Los Angeles, its City of the Dead, Los Angeles a city named for a woman, Mary, the birth mother goddess, has naturally, also her concomitant, the Great Pit of Death, whose awareness and whose memories drift into the concrete and the window-panes, the street signs and the trees and the pavement and paint and glass and rubber and air, all of the city copying itself, mating, bringing with it the shadow of Death, its own particular L.A. version, shadows hovering.

Stierlitz stands among the bones of the city, great humeruses and ulnae, skyscapers apartment buildings shopping malls grocery stores of Los Angeles—great bones—and amidst them the little bones, the people, and Stierlitz is touching little bones so delicately.

He steps into the street and traffic swerves around him, the music blaring, he is singing, in Russian, the light moving over him and through him, the beating heart of the city is revealed to him, crippling mad and dripping blood, beautiful and mad, and Stierlitz is mad, laughing mad, until he is struck by a car.

31
Hospital

Stierlitz, come with me.

Stierlitz, come with me.

Come with me into the night.

"I'm here."

Stierlitz, I love you. Do you love me?

"Yes."

Stierlitz, what am I to do? I've sold you to the highest bidder, I've bid you off into the night, to Semyonov, to what's his name. Stierlitz. Tell me. What can I do for you now?

"Tell me where I am."

You're in hospital, Stierlitz. You got hit by a car.

"Is that why I hear voices in my head?"

Yes, Stierlitz. That's why.

"Hmm."

Stierlitz. You have a mission. A mission from God.

"I do?"

Find out, Stierlitz. Find out what's happened to us. We need to know.

"How do I do that?"

If I knew I wouldn't have to ask you, Stierlitz. Find out for us. Find out for us all.

"Okay ..."

His nurse checked his monitors and changed

his bandages and his boss came to visit. Outside the light continued moving, over his bed, over his eyes. He dreamed in yellow, and red.

In one of the dreams he was the Khan's horse again, free, on the steppes of Russia, plowing the earth, moving over the grass, galloping ...

When he awoke Ekaterina was by his side.

"Where is my wife?" he asked.

"She's coming," she said, and held his hand.

Over the world mountains are singing, for Stierlitz.

Over the world, mountains are singing, for Stierlitz and his play.

Stierlitz?

Stierlitz!

Maximilian!

"Just call me Max."

The transvestite, Shaundra, was there too, dabbing at her eyes.

"Colonel, what did you do?" she asked.

"I've gone mad," said Stierlitz.

Stierlitz's wife crossed herself.

"You're not mad, Maxy," said Ekaterina. "You're just in Los Angeles."

Part 3
Los Angeles

How do you say "fuck you" in Hollywood?
"Trust me."
— traditional Los Angeles joke

32
Journeys from Los Angeles

Semyonov was standing outside the hospital when they wheeled Stierlitz out, next to a plain-clothes cop.

"Welcome back, Max," said Semyonov.

"Who's this get-up?" asked Max, pointing at the cop.

"This is Colonel Bumgarten. He'll be assisting us."

"Bumgarten," said Stierlitz.

"Nice to meet ya, Max." The man stuck out his

99

hand. Max took it. The man had a huge hand.

Stierlitz's train of women emerged from the hospital doors.

"You're Los Angeles police?" Max asked Bumgarten.

"Gentlemen," intoned Max's wife, inserting herself gently between Max and the men, "won't you come by my husband's apartment later for tea? We must get him home for his afternoon's rest."

"Really, rybka, these gentlemen are tired too. Why not tomorrow, gentlemen? Come by my office. I must greet you in bed, I'm afraid!"

"Nice looking women you've got here, Max," observed Bumgarten.

Shaundra took a step closer to Bumgarten and grinned.

"Aren't you a handsome one too?" she said.

"Get your rest, Max," said Semyonov. "You'll need it."

The women hovered over Max's bed at the hospital.

"Please, would you two run down and get some groceries for Max? Please take this." Mrs. Stierlitz handed Ekaterina and Shaundra some money.

When the women had left, Mrs. Stierlitz stood over her husband in his bed. He regarded her warily.

"How are you feeling?" she asked.

"Fine."

"He is a Colonel, that American officer?"

"Yes, with the police."

"What do they want with you, Max?"

"You've ever asked me about my work before."

"You've never acted like this before."

"You were asleep, zvyozdochka. You were asleep a long time."

"Well I'm awake now, and I want to know."

"I don't know. Semyonov claims he wants me to investigate a Swedish plot, but I can find no evidence of it. I'm trying to treat it like a vacation."

"Then do, Max! Send those other women away. Let us be together, like we used to. The children are being looked after by Mrs. Ramey."

"Mrs. Ramey? Well, that is well. I can't send those men away yet. I have discovered something else, something ... that affects all of us."

She sat down next to him on the bed.

"What is it Max?"

"These dreams you had, that sleep. I have been having it too. Some spirit is moving over the world—a demon, if you like. Or an angel. Perhaps an alien mind. Whatever it is, it's coming closer to all of us. These things that have happened—to Mother Russia, and here in America too, they have a cause, which, I believe is in outer space."

"You need to sleep, Max. I'll make tea." She kissed his forehead.

Max lay back against his pillows and closed his eyes but did not sleep. In the darkness behind his eyes, he remembered the light under Los Angeles, in the subway.

Stierlitz's mind soared over the City of Angels, the City of Messengers, tumbling in the light and shadow—lights rectilinear and framed, like the angles of a stealth bomber, like the angles of a Renaissance fortress, like the angles of Saturn's polar storm, pentagonal, orthogonal ... a Q-bert landscape of light over the city, infinite.

"Who is it threatens Moscow?" asked Stierlitz.

Is that the right question Stierlitz?

"Dammit, who are you?"

I'm just this guy, Stierlitz. I want to help you.

"Then tell me. Who threatens my city!"

I don't know any more than you do.

"You know something! Tell me!"

I only know you're part of it Stierlitz. Like the man says: look within ...

"Balls."

Dreaming, Colonel Stierlitz soared high over the Earth.

I love you, Stierlitz. And Stierlitz, I'm sorry.

"What do you mean!"

The Earth explodes. In the night, or the dark. Or in between. It happens in one part of the universe. And in the other part is Stierltiz, the eternal Stierlitz, like God, watching, spying, glimpsing us, he strange troubadour, he make big stink, he totanka, wavering his horns into the sky.

Stierlitz!

"Aaaaaaaaaaaaaaaaaaaaaaaaaaaaaaaaaaaaaaaaaaa
aaaaaaaaaa"

The Explodes in the dark night sky but it en-
dures too, in a parallel universe, and Stierlitz must
now exist in both.

You're two men Stierlitz.

You are the survivor, and the victim. The perp,
and the savage.

You are Moscow, and the Soviet Union. And
you, Stierlitz, are Our Great Democratic Hope.

Carry it lightly Stierlitz, as you carry your wom-
en, over the mountains:

...

But all of this is still not yet. As we approach
the singularity of this event, as we interrogate the
methods and madnesses and interlocutors and
perps who perpetrate these tragedies upon us,
some unwitting, and some with full foreknowl-
edge, we must assume they know much more than
we, but that we are winning—

Let us assume that we are winning. It is the only
way to go.

33
City of Night

Come into my city, any way you can. You are welcome here.

Here in the blast site.

Here in the grave.

These broken cavalcades, and these terraces, they are yours. My City of Night has many names; I will not list them here.

Some say my City is a ruin.

Some call it a palace.

It is a court.

Courtyard and court.

Like a chess board without squares.

Like a go board without crosses.

In my domains, all things that are, are now.

Stierlitz enters, feeling abandoned, in his white cloak, for he is the white knight.

He is alone in my City of Night.

And in our other corner, his woman, his younger woman, the mistress, Ekaterina, whose name, as we have said, means torture.

The knight and the torturer meet upon the destruction of Earth.

Call it 1963 gone wrong, some cataclysm.

These events are real, though they have not happened to you.

Do all real things have to happen to you? No, we know this. My job is only to narrate. Though I play a small part in this story.

These things happened.

"Where are we Max?" asked Ekaterina.

"On the moon."

"It doesn't look like the moon."

"I'm dreaming," said Stierlitz.

"Am I dreaming too?"

"I don't know. Perhaps."

She was in black, draped over stones, lying over Stierlitz like a coat. Be his coat, woman. Shelter him now from the night. Will you?

Ekaterina lies huddled over him. She looks into the night sky.

"This dream is so real, Maxy. What's happening?"

"I don't know."

She curls atop him, to look into his face. Max looks like a god, a sleepy god, far away.

"Max. What do you want with me?"

"Only you, Ekaterina. Only you."

"You will leave your wife?"

Max puts his hand atop his woman's hip.

"Don't ask me to."

"Max, I need you to tell me something. If she died, would you marry me?"

"She will not die." And he kissed her.

All things which dwell in night are lost to us, we creatures of the day—I cannot speak of them, though I would try. They are like stars.

Burning bright next to one another.

Their heat, luminous, and life-giving.

Their light, eternal.

Their life span, measured in ages.

We may measure Stierlitz in ages, his youth, and his middle age, now approaching its end.

In my domains all things which are, are now, and I hold Stierlitz's death in my palm, the death of the Earth, the rejuvenation, the cataclysm, the trust and the truth ... without Stierlitz, in this matter, I am nothing.

I need you Stierlitz.

Stierlitz cries out, in passion.

Cities burning. Life, turning to ash. Babies, clutching mothers, in the nuclear sunrise.

We who endure remember. We who endure enlist our help in our rebuilding, of the Earth, and Moon.

Come, Stierlitz. Rebuild with me.

A Titan, is Stierlitz.

With his Titaness. These great gods, made of marble, moving over the sky like puzzle pieces, articulated joints, howling mouths, burning eyes ...

Our planet is redeemed.

34
Los Angeles

Stierlitz awoke feeling rested in his bed.

He found two men standing over him.

"We have a movie ticket for you," one of them said, and they dragged him out of bed, in his pajamas.

They took him downstairs and into their black car and drove him to the movie theater.

Inside was dark and they presented their tickets to the ticket taker, who tore them, and gave them back their stubs. One of the men pushed a stub into Stierlitz's pajama pocket.

"Don't lose that," he said.

Inside the movie theater, all is a dream, and I'm sorry for that Stierlitz, this crimson river of my heart, and yours, of dream, bleeds ... and I know there is no explaining the reason for it to us, though we know it needs to be done.

"Do I know that?" muttered Stierlitz.

I don't know Stierlitz. Watch the movie.

Light blazes over the screen.

"We've been wanting to talk to you, Stierlitz," one of the men said. He wore a beard on his face.

Stierlitz regarded the man.

"When you're a man, in a prison, what is your first duty?"

"To survive," said Stierlitz, and the other man, leaned over, and held onto Stierlitz's neck, and punched him in the kidney with his other hand. Stiertliz cried out, into the darkness.

"How will you survive?" asked the bearded man.

"I'll help you," said Stierlitz.

"That is good. But why?" And the other man hit Stierlitz again, and he cried out, into the dark movie theater. On the screen, asteroids tumbled past the camera. It was a science fiction movie.

"Because you're good men," gritted Stierlitz, and he laughed, a raucous laugh, into the dark.

And the second man hit him again, for a long time, and Stierlitz blacked out.

When he awoke, aliens were talking to the astronaut on the screen, in their language. Stierlitz was not certain whether the language the men next to him were speaking was not the same.

"We're like you, Stierlitz," said the bearded man. "We're spies. Spies, from a very long way away. Do you want to come with us, Stierlitz?"

"No," said Stierlitz.

"Do you want to come with us, into outer space, Stierlitz?"

"No, I don't."

"You're going to come with us, Stierlitz. And what you're going to see will change you. And we hope that it changes you in the right way. It's going to help you. Now stand up, Stierlitz."

Stierlitz attempted to stand in the movie theater but the second man held him down.

"Can't you stand up, Stierlitz?" said the bearded

man.

Stierlitz struggled against the man holding him, who had huge hands.

"Stand up, Stierlitz," said the bearded man. "Show us what you can do."

Stierlitz tried. He could feel the second man smiling next to him, as he bore down on him with his weight.

"You're going to take a pill, Stierlitz. And when you awake you will be in a far away place. Do you understand?"

"No," said Stierlitz.

"And in that place you will be ours, Stierlitz. You will need to listen to us. Because, although we mean you harm, we also mean for you to survive. And the others, they don't. Do you understand?"

"Yes."

"Open wide."

Stierlitz did.

He swallowed the pill. It tasted bitter. On screen, the aliens appeared to be eating the astronaut; that is, they clustered over him, sucking on the man's body with their many mouths. Perhaps it was a sexual initiation. It filled Stierlitz with revulsion.

"My wife ..." muttered Stierlitz.

"She's going to be fine," whispered the bearded man. "Sleep, Stierlitz. And when you awake, listen for the sound of my voice."

All things attend to the mission. What we have sent, may be delivered. And the message it carries, is the world.

Stierlitz, attend to the sound of my voice.

"I'm going to fucking murder you, asshole."

I know, Stierlitz. On the count of ten, you will be awake. You will need to pay attention then as you will be in some danger.

One.

Two.

Three.

"Where is it I am going?"

I don't know any more than you do Stierlitz. I'm sorry. Four.

"Tell my wife ... that I love her."

She knows, Stierlitz. You're a good man. Five. Six. Seven. Eight.

"I remember something."

Nine.

"I remember who I'm supposed to be ..."

Ten. You're awake, Stierlitz. Guard yourself.

35
Torture

He's in a tree; he can feel it swaying. He's in a hammock, or a creche. The arms reach in and stick him with the electrodes. His body spasms.

After a time it stops and he stares into the foreign sun.

He leans over the edge of the hammock, and grips the edge of it with his hands, and swings out of the hammock, but his muscles can't support his weight, and he drops, below, onto the dark grass.

You've really done it this time Stierlitz, he thinks.

Some distance away from him is a huge vole-like creature, with dark fur and dark eyes. It regards him silently.

Stierlitz tries to speak but all that comes out is "uhhhhh."

"Uhhhhhh. Uhhhhhh," says Stierlitz.

The vole-creature regards him steadily.

Perhaps it is friendly, he thinks. Stierlitz moves his head and makes the sound again, "Uuhhhh. Uhhhhh." The vole-creature takes a step towards him. Stierltiz can see that tentacles dangle from its belly. One of the tentacles appears to be made of metal.

"Uhhh," says Stierlitz, smiling crazily. He manages to sit up on one elbow. The creature comes closer. Then it makes a high pitched sound, horrific in intensity. Stierlitz collapses back onto the dark grass and holds his hands over his ears.

He manages to pry his eyes open to look at the creature, which is still making the sound. "Uhh! Uhhhhhh!" says Stierlitz through his flapping mouth, like a half-dead muscle, and the thing stops.

"Uh!" says Stierlitz. The thing regards him. Stierlitz makes a move towards the creature, moving through the grass.

I CAN SEE YOU says the voice in Stierlitz's head. It is the man with the beard, from the movie theater.

"Uh! Uh!" says Stierltiz to the creature, and its metal tentacle wraps around Stierlitz's body, and drags him onto its back. Stierlitz grips its stange, stinky fur, and looks around at the alien world.

They are moving.

KILL THIS THING. EAT IT. says the voice.

Stierlitz grips its fur. Over the sky, ships are arriving. They bear the signs of the Soviet Empire, hammer and sickle. They also bear the insignia of the American Empire, the snake, and its thirteen satellites.

The ships streak red and gold over the silver sky and Stierlitz finds himself laughing, and the vole is moving faster, squeaking.

I love you, woman, thinks Stierlitz, and he does not even know which woman he means. Perhaps the idea of woman.

STIERLITZ ARE YOU THERE?

I'm here, thinks Stierlitz.

I THOUGHT I'D LOST YOU. OUR BEAM IS CURVING AROUND SOME ASTRAL BODIES. HOLD STILL A MOMENT.

"Fast," whispers Stierlitz, into the vole's ear, and it does, moving through the dark lustrous grass towards the ships, now landing. Astronauts are grappling down from the ships.

He holds tight to the vole.

Stierlitz, are you all right? I love you, mother-fucker.

Stierlitz clutches the animal, and whispers to it.

STIERLITZ, KILL THIS BEAST.

Stierlitz is a bear.

Man bear.

Bear man.

He whispers to the animal under his body.

All of the electrons of his passage surge through the air around him.

"Good boy," says Stierlitz.

They approach the astronauts.

"I am Russian, Comrade!" shouts Stierlitz at the nearest man, who raises his rifle.

Stierlitz dismounts from the animal.

"Welcome to my planet!" Stierlitz announces. He waves enthusiastically.

The astronaut lowers his rifle a tad.

The torture is back, through the sky¬—Stierlitz sees it as a field of energy, black on white, lightning in balls searing through dimensions. It attaches itself onto the craft and Stierlitz imagines he can hear the astronauts scream, though there is no sound.

Stierlitz runs for the man with the rifle and tackles him, seizing the rifle, and then grabbing the astronaut's hand he runs back towards the animal. He gestures for the astronaut to get on. Behind them, the torture is eating the ship. Stierlitz can really hear the screams now; it sounds like buzzing.

The astronaut climbs on the animal. Stierlitz behind.

"Take us home, boy," Stierlitz says, and the animal runs.

Over the dark grass twin suns are circling. Stierlitz holds the animal. He is Genghis Khan. Beneath him, his mount. Around him, the universe.

"I'm sorry about your friends," Stierlitz says, but the astronaut does not seem to hear. He taps the man on the shoulder, and gestures for him to remove his helmet.

He does. He looks like a Swede, with blonde hair, and Aryan features. But he does not speak Swedish. The man shouts with great emotion. Stierlitz nods, and points ahead, to indicate they are going home.

I SEE THAT YOU ARE A GREAT SPY, STIER-LITZ. TELL US, WHAT DO YOU SEE?

Stierlitz looks up at the great silver sky. He has never seen anything like it. There are so many moons; seven at least. No, eight. The planet must be huge.

He has traveled into the future, Stierlitz decides. The great American Empire and the great Soviet Empire have joined forces to conquer the galaxy. With the Swedes, it seems. Amazing. How could Moscow decide to work with Stockholm? Something must have happened. Once he learns the language of the astronaut he will have to question him.

They arrive in a valley in the dark steppe, the animal's tribe is nesting there. Eating the dark grass. Stierlitz and the astronaut dismount, and the animal begins to feed, and nuzzles one of its mates.

Stierlitz knows the torture will come back. He grabs the astronaut's shoulder, points at the sky, and then the ground, to indicate they should build a shelter.

They grab rocks and dig into the earth.

All mammals remember the earth. Beneath her shelter there is salvation. (From asteroids!) From torture monsters of all kinds.

It is dark and the animal comes to say goodnight. They continue to dig, hollowing out a small hole. When they have dug enough to be out of a complete sight line with the sky, they collapse, and nurse their bleeding fingers. They sleep next to one another, like brothers.

In the dark shelter Stierlitz is at a kind of peace. Revolving silently about the orbit of his mind.

Outside, the Torture is waiting.

Inside, he regards himself as a scientist might regard the nervous system of a heretofore undiscovered species of jellyfish: as a system to be probed and understood.

He is sinking in to himself. Into the dark water.

Outside, he can hear the sounds, of The Torture. The astronaut is rolling his body, mumbling, in his sleep.

Stierlitz feels the deep and solemn quiet.

He opens his eyes on the dark.

HELLO STIERLITZ

He listens inside his own brain, for the command, the word, the name, of the power he needs. A name for what, and who he is now. He can't find it.

STIERLITZ, PLEASE KILL THIS ASTRONAUT.

Stierlitz goes outside. Immediately the Torture attaches itself to him, scaring off the herd of great voles. The vines and wires of the Torture bind themselves to his nerves and begin to apply the electricity.

Silently, he is screaming. He opens his mouth, gaping to the night sky full of aliens stars.

The pain is good because it scares away the terrible voice.

Who am I, he thinks. Am I still Russian?

He is rowing. Rus, which means row, in his longboat.

His beard has grown full. Success in Anatolia. Now, for the Great Steppes of the East ...

Stierlitz imagines his Viking ancestor. As the Torture feeds on him, he twitches, imagining his arms and stroking through the water with his oars.

After a time the Torture receeds, and Stierlitz staggers to the river to wash himself, and to spit up the blood.

A New Russian stops his Mercedes 600 at a red light. With screeching brakes a Zaprozhets approaches and rear-ends it. The New Russian gets out of his Mercedes and approaches the Zaprozhets. Behind the wheel is a meek little man, looking in great fear at the New Russian.

- Don't be afraid, says the New Russian. Just tell me one thing: how do you stop at the light when I am not there?

-- traditional Russian joke

36
Ekaterina Dreaming

What Russian woman has not dreamed of the great night, and its men?

She is sleeping in her slip. The night air is blowing over her.

She picks up the telephone.

"Maxy? Is it you?"

There is no one on the other end of the telephone. She hangs up.

She goes out onto the fire escape. Moscow is one long system of interconnected fire escapes. One can escape fire; one cannot escape Moscow.

Ektaterina, whose name means Torturer, has Jewish ancestors, and carries proudly their great stubbornness. Though, how one can distinguish between Russian and Jewish stubbornness, I am not sure.

She lights a cigarette.

Above her Stierlitz's spirit founders, a will-o-wisp. She sees it but she ignores it, like any good Gypsy princess. Like any Russian czarina.

Spirits may wait, on nicotine.

"What is it?" she asks, craftly, staring into the face of his spirit.

The white smoke of his face makes a wide 'O.' 'Come to me,' his lips seem to say.

"Again?" she says, looking at him. "What about what happened last time?"

'Please' the lips seem to say.

"Oh Maxy. I'll be so old. So old by the time you are really mine!"

I know.

She flies into the night. Some dark storm's coming, czarina, be careful, will you?

"Shut up, I can fly this thing myself."

Czarina, won't you let me help you?

"Help, from an American? Pshah."

Czarina fly. over the great western expanse of night, through heliosphere, to the infinite:

Tell me who has heard your voice, shouted through the nights of all of us, little darling, when you were asleep crowding your voice out, against all that was, and all that would be? It was you, Torturer, head-bound against the night, stirring your deadly name out against the sky.

She is spinning.

Over Moscow.

Inside my heart.

Stierlitz is vomiting into the black river.

She arrives. Singing soft and low, like a dream.

Ekaterina and the astronaut lead Stierlitz towards the voles.

They are moving towards the Khan's great herd.

Soon they will have names.

Ekaterina chants hers, a word untranscribable, wind:

And the men climb on beside her, bound north, over the great planet, to hunt the astronaut's ship.

To save Russia.

To find Stalin's grave secret.

The beasts feel their great purpose and increase their speed.

Ekaterina's slip shines white and luminous; her blood hot enough to keep her warm for the riding.

Torture is twisting, and as Saint Catherine spins upon her wheel the arc of torture admits no defeat, only tighter spirals:

Over them, white ghosts, tendrils, stretch themselves over the black sky, blanking out the stars.

"Faster!" cries Ekaterina, and they do.

They see the ghost ship then; white as the spirit tendrils, a troop transport made to cross light years now slipped into some dimension near death. Blazing white banner.

"Aiii!" cries the astronaut, his face in horror.

Stierlitz, with great energy, vaults to a neighboring steed and accelerates toward the ghost ship. Icy white tendrils from the sky sweep down over him, pursuing him as roots pursue water.

The tendrils lift him into the air; into the sky.

Ekaterina cries his name, and she and the astronaut accelerate, chasing him, as he is swept up towards the ship.

"More Russian ghosts," mutters Stierlitz, as he is pulled towards the leering entrance of the ship. "I should have brought my holy water."

He is brought into the ship; the white metal walls are dim compared to the luminous spirits, hovering along the walls.

At the end of the hall a darker spirit hovers, his face grim.

"Let me tell you a story," begins Stierlitz, in his best schoolmaster voice. "Long ago I was a boy on a ship, bound for Kaliningrad, with my mother. In those days many Russians took sea journeys, before airplanes had been invented, or space travel.

"The vessel on which my mother and I traveled encountered a storm, and I was carried up into it, much as I have been carried into your ship. You believe that you are the terrors and rulers of this isle¬—this planet—but you are not. The planet is not yours. And I will tell you why."

All this while Stierlitz had been advancing towards the dark ghost, who regarded Stierlitz with a sneer. At this point the ghost attacked, throwing all into delirium in the passageway: no direction any longer had the same meaning, nor was it clear at which point one body separated from another.

We derive our identity in large part from that which lies beneath us (the word 'subject' 's literal meaning). But we also derive it from that which lies before us (the word 'object.')

Any dreamer knows the distinction between subject and object can become blurry¬—between self and other. In such moments it is—though not entirely—the will that determines what new boundaries will be drawn.

Stierlitz felt his arm reach out, across skies numberless, near infinite, as though his joints were planets, and his eyes stars. The dark spirit moved around him, a fluid, a cloud bank, rings, after rings, after rings, circling him, binding him. He cried out, his voice nuclear fuel, burning, igniting, setting suns alight.

Set suns alight, Stierlitz. There's a good lad. Always more where those came from.

Ekaterina and the astronaut threw themselves from the backs of the great voles into the trailing wisps, like ropes, which seized them, sluggishly, and they gripped the glowing weeds tightly in their fists, and began to climb up towards the ghost ship.

She climbed aboard the ship, through the open door. White spirits cluttered the passage. At the end of it Stierlitz lay on the floor, entangled in a black ghost who looked like a man. She ran to him, knelt and gripped his shoulders, shaking him, horrified. The dark ghost moved over him like bitter liquid.

"Maxy! Wake up! Wake up!"

Stierlitz. Have you identified the threat?

I am the threat, thought Stierlitz.

No, Max. Not you. Who is it, Max? Tell me?

I don't know ...

Find out, Max.

"Wake up!" she shouted. Behind her, the astronaut had removed a device from his waist, a small cylinder. He began to spray the ghosts with it, and the ship trembled. Around Max, the black spirit became angrier, spinning about him like a desperate spider.

Max's eyes snapped open.

"I am in the clouds," he said.

"You're with me, Max," Kat said. "I'm here." She pressed her hand to his face.

"Mother has left," Max said.

"Stay with me, Max. I'm not leaving."

Then the black spirit contracted, like a Chinese finger trap, coating Max's body like a fatal glove. Ekaterina screamed.

37
Decisions

Semyonov is playing with the old fashioned telephone in his office. Considering whether to dial.

The Worker sleeps in his tree.

Mohammed is climbing aboard the rocket ship. A stowaway.

The astronaut knelt at Ekaterina's side, took out his knife, and cut the black over Stierlitz, drawing blood.

Stierlitz dreams. I am dreaming too.

Semyonov dials the number.

It's ringing.

It's ringing.

It's ringing.

38
Stierlitz's Dream

The Khan smelled meat; a fire. He knelt lower over his mount and whispered into its ear; Stierlitz ran faster, towards the hill.

Atop the hill they could see the setting sun slipping over the blue-grey ridges in the distance. The fire was visible below.

"Go, sweet," whispered the Khan, and Stierlitz rode into the darkening grass, alone, and the Khan descended on foot to greet the party.

With his right eye Stierlitz watched the Khan. Stierlitz bowed, chewing grass. The fire played over the Khan's armor as the men and women at the fire stood at his approach. Stierlitz watched them.

Above them a streak of white fire through the sky. They raised their eyes to look.

Stierlitz, startled, took off over the field, running, and running.

Inside his mind a telephone was ringing.

STIERLITZ WAKE UP

The phone call was not important. The Khan was important. The Khan loved Stierlitz. He loved the Khan. Though he knew they would one day be separated.

Stierlitz wanted to see the sun again and so he rode, fast, to the blue-grey ridges, to catch it.

Somewhere inside him he felt something growing. A memory, or a curse.

The Khan loves me, Stierlitz thought. I must do something for him. I must bring him more horses.

Stierlitz rode down over the ridge. He smelled his kind some miles distant.

Stierlitz ... be careful. Will you?

I'm riding.

That's not all you're doing.

Yes, it is.

Stierlitz rode, into the darkening night. The stars lit the paths of the horses; but he was following his nose.

At last he broke into them, speaking, in the language of horses in his dream.

They left together, towards the Khan.

"What is it you want to do with him?" asked one of the other man horses.

"Help him," said Stierlitz.

"Why?"

"He loves me."

"So do we."

"The Khan is a great man, with many friends."

"Too many friends is dangerous," the man horse said.

Stierlitz said nothing. They rode, until it was light.

The party had not seen the wisdom of the Khan's mission. He departed alone, hailing Stierlitz from the hilltop, grinning at all the new horses he had brought.

They rode north, all together, into the mountains.

Above them the dark spirit moved, counting the sounds of the phone.

one two three four five
STIERLITZ YOU HAVE TO GET OUT OF THERE

Listen to him Stierlitz. You can't stay there forever.

The phone is ringing.

Ring

Ring

Ring

39
Los Angeles

Stierlitz's wife picks up the telephone.

"Hello?"

"Mrs. Stierlitz, this is Semyonov."

"Yes?"

In the forest outside Moscow, the Worker awoke in his tree.

In the Stierlitz family apartment, Mrs. Stierlitz clutched the telephone.

"Max is dead, Mrs. Stierlitz. I'm so sorry."

"What? What do you mean? He's in Los Angeles!"

"I just received word from the Kremlin. I don't know all the details yet. Stay put. I am coming to America. What Max was involved in concerns the state. Will you wait for me?"

Mrs. Stierlitz dropped the phone. She began to scream.

In Russia, from his tree, the Worker dropped, soft on his feet. He was going to see the old wise woman in the wood.

40
Dream Steppes

Max felt something in him; he neighed. It was the curse.

Was this what got Stalin? he wondered. This alien curse ...

I need to wake up, Stierlitz thought.

The phone has stopped ringing, Max. I'm not sure you can wake up now.

I will wake up.

Then do it.

Max the horse blinked his eyes. Around him the steppes spun. The Khan was saying something to him, concern on his face. The other horses scattered. Overhead, the white fire stretched over the sky, the landing craft.

I will wake up.

Do it, Max!

I will wake the world.

Then do it.

These frequencies of mine, so vulnerable, bent subtle in and under, the wide and startling night:

Stierlitz bolts, away from the Great Khan (not yet emperor of China), away from his fellow horses, into the steppes of dream.

If no one will know, Stierlitz, I still will. Stierlitz, tell me, tell me, what is it you want?

I want Semyonov here, so I can beat his ass.

Your wish is my command, Stierlitz. Go gentle

on him, hey, he doesn't have your experience.

I'm going to beat him within an inch of his life!

Shake rattle and roll: take control, and flow me, know me, sold me for a wave, in the dark, Stierlitz! Stierlitz, did you sell me for a wave in the dark?!

I don't know.

He's coming Stierlitz! He's coming!

Gargantuan supreme, a king:

Semyonov weighing in at 3,200 kilos, at fifteen foot eight inches, battling Colonel Maximilian Stierlitz, Defender of the Rus, madman, cloak and dagger man, in the steppes no one knows your name, all they know is how you can handle your horse:

David and Goliath. Servant and master.

The lithe limbed plumber of the Russian conscience Yulian Semyonov, muscles rippling, skin shining in the sun, lets out a great roar over the plains:

"Aaaaaaaaaaaaaaaghh!"

Stierlitz is laughing, running, horse and man, luring the beast to a cliff.

"I'll kill you, Semyonov! You've had it coming! And when I've got you, I'm coming for you, Robin!"

All right, Stierlitz. Come down.

He runs, madman, arc of the long divide of history, his spycraft like no other, his ways, the ways of a soldier, his eyes, long and sad and Russian—how else could they be?—his soul, water, flowing, up:

flowing up:

"Come for me, Semyonov!" he cries, wielding his blade, and Semyonov does, his great fists pumping the air, and swinging:

Inside the Torture Ship Stierlitz awakes, black spirit shining over his body, and he lurches forward:

"I must get to the control room," he says.

"Come!" Ekaterina says, and she and the astronaut hold him as they walk, slow, through the trembling vessel. Stierlitz eyes flutter.

"I'm still in the steppe," he mutters.

"Come, Maxy, we're getting you there!"

Stierlitz drives the blade into Semyonov's gut.
In his office in Moscow, Semyonov collapses.

Stierlitz touches the controls and the black spirit shimmers off his fingers into the console, flickering madly.

"I am in control of the vessel," says Stierlitz. "Semyonov is dead."

"Max, the spirit. It's still in you."

"I know."

"My comrades, are they dead?" said the astronaut.

"I fear so. Please, help me pilot this hunk of bolts." Black fire continued to shimmer over Stierlitz's body.

The astronaut took the co-pilot's seat.

"We will return to Earth," announced Stierlitz.

"Where is that?" asked the astronaut.

41
Interstellar Flight

Czar czarina fly, my hairy ones (for Caesar means "hairy"), endowed with the mystery of interstellar travel, endure the worst and bring these seasons near to our own:

Tell us (your lightest word will be treasured), what is the secret of your contentment? And what the secret of your discontent? What continents are moved by thee?

(For they shall spirit us away, our thousand princes princesses inside our souls, ancestral and their echoes in the future, inelectuable but growing kinder ...)

Grow kinder yet, Stierlitz! The Great Khan remembers you!

Where is he?

Inside your heart, Stierlitz!

I'm coming for you, Robin.

In space, no one will remember you—at least, not within the arc of the human imagination. Space will remember you. We will remember. But we are older than humanity; we are what humanity was and will be (and is), these times:

These times swirl and the vessels of our find trio and our mad Muslim fighter, unconquerable, divested of earthly troubles, meet in the void to reconnoiter.

A ship from the past and a ship from the the future meet in their present, outside the orbit of Saturn.

Stierlitz rests his hand on Ekaterina's shoulder. Torturess, feel right; torturess, know the moment; torturess, endure:

42
Saturn

Russia may colonize the galaxy but still she must come to understanding about her roots: what makes her tick, what makes her shrink and grow, what gods orbit her strange arc, what choices did she make, now almost forgotten?

The airlock cycled through Mohammed.

"What is he doing here?" asked Stierlitz.

"He came after me ..." said Ekaterina.

Stierlitz looked out of the window at the tiny blue spark of Earth. Russia was within him, but also there, inside that blue.

"We'll make him his berth."

Mohammed looked exhausted. Ekaterina and Stierlitz held him, while the astronaut made a bed for him. He fell asleep quickly. They turned off the light, and settled over whiskey at the galley table.

"I haven't yet identified the threat to Mother Russia," said Stierlitz.

"Maybe it's you, Max. Maybe you're the threat to Mother Russia."

"If I am I should not return."

"Then let's go to the moon, Max. Let's die together on the moon."

She embraced him, and stroked his cheek.

"Yes, Max?" she said.

"I would gladly die on the moon with you, Kat."
She kissed him.

Mohammed glared out of the porthole at Saturn's rings. He felt very far away. He was glad to be rid of his fishing vessel, in truth. But now he had harnessed himself with another vessel.

This Russian woman was insane. Perhaps all Russians were insane. But she was beautiful. A terrible shame, her being so beautiful. And him so vulnerable to beauty.

Stierlitz dreamed.

43
Stierlitz's Dream

Ekaterina was flying over the fishing vessel. Stierlitz flew over her. He watched her land on it, and embrace the Indian man on board.

Stierlitz soared higher, and Huginn and Muginn alit on his shoulders.

"Where is Odin, brothers?"

"You are he," said Muginn.

"My woman is cheating on me," said Stierlitz.

"You have worse problems than that," said Huginn. "Stalin is still alive."

"What do you mean?" asked Stierlitz.

"I have seen him in the woods."

"What is he doing?"

"He is eating."

"What does the thing eat?"

"He is eating birds, Max. He is eating my people."

"Bring me to him," said Max.

They flew into the storm, and the lightning coarsed over their bodies like runnelets of blood over a warm sword.

44
The Old Woman

Baba Yaga, as she called herself sometimes, to the children's amusement, was preparing her potion.

And she laughed into the sky, to fulfill her role, as the witch.

In the forest, some of the children howled with her.

Brezhnev has died, but his body lives on.

-- traditional Russian joke

45
Stalin, again

"What are you?" asked Stierlitz, looking at the black body, the black tar body, the tar baby, the thing, hugging the tree, with its wide eyes.

"I am this thing called Russia," said the thing who had been Stalin.

"I destroyed you," said Stierlitz.

Huginn crawed on his shoulder.

"I don't remember," said the thing, its eyes wide. "I'm hungry."

Stierlitz took out his handgun, aiming at the thing's head. He fired, and the bullet penetrated the thing's head, but the tarbaby head swallowed the bullet, and the thing moved away, loping like a low ape, and growling.

"When will it finally die?" asked Stierlitz.

"When Russia dies, Max," said Huginn.

"Am I dreaming?"

"You're awake, Max," said Muginn. "We are the ones who are dreaming."

"I must defeat this evil. It threatens Mother Russia."

"But it is Russia, Max. The thing is Russia."

"I want my banjo," said Max.
The ravens fluttered their feathers.
"Let us fly," said Max, and they took into the air.

46
Robin

"What are you doing?"

"Writing you, Stierlitz. I'm writing you."

"What am I up to?"

"I guess you're defeating evil. You seem fond of that," I said.

"You're evil, Robin."

"Evil enough, Max. Evil enough. You too."

Part 4
The Desert

"I flunked my history exam, Petka. They asked me who Caesar was, and I said it's a stallion from our 7th cavalry squadron."

"It's all my fault, Vasily Ivanovich! While you were away, I reassigned him to the 6th!"

—traditional Russian joke

47
Mountain

He could see his hands in the light, white and shining. The horizon was yellow, and blue.

The sand felt solid under his feet.

He waved his hand in front of his face, as though to check that it were real. So bright in the light.

He moved forward into the desert.

Once, he had been in Russia. Some place that was like this, but also very different.

Those thoughts were far away.

Ahead of him, a grotto of sand beckoned him in, a kind of art gallery of strange shapes made from rock and yucca.

He moved in closer, feeling the heat on his face.

In the grotto he began to sweat, and wiped the moisture from his forehead.

Somewhere inside his head he heard a kind of whisper, like a mouse out after dark, speaking into the night air some secret that was lost to the sand and the stars.

He moved over by a rock into a scrap of shade, next to a yucca. He sat down, the sand surprisingly cool against his pants. He looked at the sky, blue and white.

His feet were well shod, new leather.

On his finger, a ring. Gold, with letters written on it.

He wanted to speak a word, to the world here. He smiled, into the heat.

He felt the word would come to him. He laughed a little to himself.

He worried that he might be insane.

"This is the desert," he said. The grotto around him and the heat beyond it were not impressed by his words.

He was remembering. He'd been dreaming. A very long and complicated dream. He leaned back against the rock and reached into his backpack. He took out his metal canteen and drank from it, enjoying the metallic taste it gave to the water.

A shimmering haze moved over the yuccas in the near distance.

He turned his head, looking north. There was a rock there. It looked closer than it was. Large, and black. Volcanic. A sign. He would go there. But he should wait until dark.

In the day, the heat could kill him. He clung to his scrap of shade, watching the life around him.

He watched it for hours. Eventually the sun started to go down, and it got cool. He put on his jacket, a blue polyester windbreaker that rustled when he moved.

The mountains were far away. Stierlitz sat by the rock and watched them. They leered at him, strange dark women on the horizon. He smiled back. His teeth were weapons. He laughed at the horizon.

"I am not nobody. I am the protector of the land! I breathe fire! I can fly! I am a dragon! Haha-hahahahahah!"

The mountains kept watching him.

When it was dark Stierlitz began to walk towards them. Drawn like a string over the carpet towards the cat's mouth.

The darkness was rich and full, a thousand colors of darkness. He moved carefully through it, watching his water, and the mountains.

The desert at night was more beautiful than anything Stierlitz could describe. It did not matter to him how he had come to be there. It did not matter if he was only a dream. He was real enough to be here, in the dark.

There were sparks, in the sky.

An attack? thought Stierlitz. No, they were only meteors.

He was delirious, he realized. Delirious from beauty. He was in a painting. This grand and beautiful dark light desert painting black violet colors—he shut his eyes.

He listened to his feet on the rough sand.

When he opened his eyes he was closer to the mountains. It was getting light.

He remembered now the Los Angeles subway. The light had moved into him. Had translated him into something.

It was inside him, whatever it was. Like an organ. Like a new kind of blood.

Moments before the sun pierced the horizon he took shelter by the rocks, digging a shallow hole, to cool his sweating body.

He sipped his water and examined the surface of the rock. There was something written into it; scratched into it with a knife.

HERE THERE BE DRAGONS it said.

Stierlitz smiled with wide eyes. He peeked over the rock at the mountain above him.

"Dragons?" he whispered. He laughed, quietly.

He slept as the sun rose.

When it was dark again he climbed the mountain. The rocks were sharp against his skin; he began to bleed. He kept climbing.

He had climbed rocks as a boy, and he remembered the psychology of it, the patience.

He made good time but the peak was still an hour or so away when the sun began to rise again. He was near exhaustion.

He closed his eyes again and dreams came.

"Max?"

"Darling."

"Max?"

It was Ekaterina's voice.

"Kat."

"Max!"

He saw the face of the gnome. Grinning. It was speaking with Ekaterina's voice.

"Stierlitz."

"It's you, gnome."

"Come with me."

"Yes, gnome."

He followed the diminuitive fellow into its cave.

"Welcome, Stierlitz," said the gnome, smiling.

"I did not thank you properly before, gnome. Please, accept my gratitude, and the honor of my family. I am in your debt."

"I helped you becauase you needed it, Stierlitz. But also because I needed something. The dragon, you're going to meet him tomorrow."

"All right."

"This dragon, you must tell him something for me."

Stierlitz nodded.

"Tell him I want away from here. I want to go to Hollywood. There's work for there, as a gnome. I'm tired of guarding his mountain. Will you tell him that, Stierlitz? He won't listen to me anymore."

"I'll tell him."

They ate a rabbit together, over the gnome's small fire.

Stierlitz was awake. It was sunset again. He tasted the rabbit fat on his lips. Delicious.

His body was stiff with exhaustion and cold. In the gathering darkness he rose again to his feet and began the climb to the peak.

He could see the shimmers at the top: the shape of the dragon. Over him the darkening sky filled him with expectation.

He reached the top and sat down on the rock. The view of the desert was beautiful. Blue grey yellow sand dimming in the fading light, stretched for a hundred miles round the peak.

He looked at his hand and saw that it was also a claw. But it was still his hand too. And inside his mouth were fangs, though they were also still his teeth.

On his back, invisible great wings.

He breathed in the dry, delicious desert air, and he exhaled, which was his fiery life.

I am a dragon, thought Stierlitz. Perhaps I have always been.

He took a drink from his water. Then he went back down the mountain to speak to the gnome. It was difficult to descend, as it had been to ascend, but faster.

He found the gnome in his cave.

"I am a dragon now," said Stierlitz.

"What?" said the gnome.

"The dragon. It's me."

"You're crazy, Stierlitz. What's the matter with you?"

"I'm telling you, I'm the dragon!" His voice came out like a roar.

"There's no need to shout," said the gnome. "If you're the dragon then take me to Hollywood. This desert is no place for a gnome."

"That's why I came, gnome. I will take you there. Let's go."

Stierlitz took the gnome onto his back, as he had once taken Genghis Khan, in his dream.

They descended the mountain and headed out across the desert.

The gnome sang a song.

"I was an eye when I was a boy;
I looked everywhere!
I was an eye when I was a boy;
I saw! I saw!
The Billingduns Man he was there in the street

The Billingduns Man he was there in the street
But I, I could not run!
No I, I could not run!
I was an eye!"

48
Walking

Stierlitz was in the desert on an important assignment from the Kremlin. He remembered now. The Kremlin had assigned him to gather intelligence on the desert and study Russia's enemies who dwelt within it.

"I am on a top secret assignment, gnome," Stierlitz told the gnome on his shoulders.

"Yes," said the gnome.

"If I do anything strange, please understand that it is part of my duties to my country. But I still plan to get you to Hollywood. That is a private matter, you understand?"

"Yes, fine, Stierlitz. What are we going to have for lunch?"

"Perhaps a cactus."

"Can we have a fire?"

"Cactus is better uncooked."

"Hmm. Perhaps I had better shoot us a bird."

"Good luck with that," said Stierlitz, chuckling.

"I am the best shot in my home county," said the gnome, growing angry.

"Don't get angry, gnome, or I will put you down."

The gnome shut up. But he still growled, faintly.

It was growing light.

"Let's eat a cactus and then go to sleep," said Stierlitz.

The gnome hopped down and went at one of the cactus with his axe. They plucked spines from the thing, hissing when one bit into their fingers. The flesh of the cactus was succulent and moist.

"Mmm," said the gnome. Stierlitz agreed.

After they had eaten the gnome pitched his small tent, and Stierlitz slept beneath it, in a hole.

Before he fell asleep he noticed he was growing scales on his body, but then remembered it was just dry skin.

When Stierlitz awoke the gnome was gone.

"Gnome!" he cried out. But there was no one there.

Where could he have gone. There's nothing else out here.

Everything suddenly seemed oppressive. Could the cactus have poisoned him? But Stierlitz himself felt fine. But what if gnomes had completely different digestive systems? That would stand to reason.

He must have offended the gnome somehow, with one of his jokes. He'd tried a few of his Russian jokes and the gnome hadn't laughed.

The desert was suddenly immense. His wings itched; he scratched them with his hand, continuing to walk into the evening.

Without the gnome's tent he would have no shelter come daylight. Perhaps he could bury himself under the sand, and breathe with a straw? He did not like that idea.

In the distance he could make out a plume of dust. Someone was approaching.

It was a desert vehicle—a four-wheeler.

It roared across the desert; although, in the way of deserts, its approach took longer than expected.

He could see it was a woman driving it. She drove fast right up to him and braked.

"Colonel Stierlitz, I presume?" shouted the old biddy over the motor. She was a madwoman.

"Who are you?" Stierlitz shouted.

"Get in! We should follow the gnome!"

"What?"

"Get in!"

Stierlitz got in and they took off across the desert.

"I've been tracking you for a while, Stierlitz!"

"Who did you say you were?" shouted Stierlitz. The woman drove like a maniac. Stierlitz braced himself against the improvised struts in the passenger cage as they lurched across the sand flat.

"I'm the old woman in the woods."

"You're friends with The Worker!" shouted Stierlitz.

She grinned, and nodded. She still had all her teeth, though several were crooked.

"How is the Worker!"

"Not so good! Worse since your last mission, Stierlitz!"

"What's the matter with him!"

"He can't get high!"

They were approaching the next set of mountains.

"Why not!" shouted Stierlitz.

"I don't know!"

Stierlitz shut his mouth; it hurt to talk over the noise. He concentrated on holding on, and keeping his eyes peeled for the gnome.

The woman was Baba Yaga, he knew. She made him feel at home.

Baba Yaga laughed at the sky, a madwoman. Stierlitz smiled too. Her face was strange, but inviting.

"How did you get here?" he asked.

"You needed me," she said.

"Yes, but how?"

"Must an old woman reveal all her secrets?"

Stierlitz watched the desert landscape.

All that he seemed to still know continued to work for him, Stierlitz realized. Despite all the strangeness he had come into.

He understood less and less, and yet felt more and more comfortable. The world conspired to lead him in the right way. Or was this feeling a false suspicion? No, he still loved Russia. It was inside him.

"Is the gnome all right?" asked Stierlitz.

"We'll find out, won't we," said the old woman, as she accelerated up a sand dune.

As they reached its crest, Stierlitz thought he

saw the little man, out towards the horizon.

"There!" The old woman looked.

"You've younger eyes," she said. "Did you see him?"

Stierlitz hesitated. "No."

"I'll need to use the gnome detector," said Baba Yaga. She took a small bag out of her satchel and unstrapped herself from the cab.

She opened the bag on the desert sand and a small robot hopped out. It extended an antenna from its cylindrical head. The antenna rotated, making a whining sound. On the face of the robot, its screen, the word 'gnome' flashed in red.

"It's there," the old woman said, pointing in a different direction than the one Stierlitz thought he had seen him.

The robot beeped.

"How can the robot know?" asked Stierlitz. "It has GPS?"

"It smells him," she said. "Come on."

They were off across the desert, wind blowing in Stierlitz's face.

49
Walking

Stierlitz is asleep. The night wind moves over the cab. His eyes snap open.

The old woman is gone. The metal of the cab is cold. The desert is beautiful, shaded in dark blue. The holy desert.

He is alone again.

What have you done, Stierlitz, he thinks. You're slipping.

Far off there is a night bird.

He touches the radio in the cab. Static.

He turns the dial, slowly. One muffled voice.

" ... the triumphant ... reveal ... hierophant ..."

Stierlitz turns on his fine spy mind and the rest of the world recedes. He parses the data of the radio.

After half an hour, he knows what he must do. In the trunk of the ATV there is a rifle. Stierlitz checks and it is loaded. He swings it over his shoulder and heads once more into the night desert, towards the hill where he originally saw the gnome for an instant. His shoes feel good on his feet; thank god he bought new ones this year. Ahead, he can hear the night bird.

Semyonov is awake. The alarm has stopped ringing. He can smell his wife cooking breakfast in the kitchen. Outside is Moscow.

Something has gone wrong. Of all of the finest orders—exquisite logics—the rules, beliefs, political equations he believed in, executed, maintained and defended, orthodox and otherwise, none have delivered the goal.

Delivered security for Russia, yes. Destroyed enemies, yes. Plots, counterplots, revolutions, all real and worthwhile.

And the ones pertaining to Stierlitz, his most valuable asset, these too have been good, useful, effective. The Motherland is secure—more, thriving.

But, simultaneously, everything has gone wrong. A spiritual malaise? Nothing so satisfying. The goal, for Semyonov, has always been death.

But Russia will not let him die. It is keeping him alive. Now he realizes this.

He could throw himself out of his window in horror. But he remembers: this is why he became a spy. To manage the existential horror.

He picks up the telephone and dials The Worker.

"Semyonov," says The Worker. "You're alive."

Semyonov sighs. "Where is Stierlitz?" he asks.

"I don't know. I'm just sitting here in my tree."

"Do you ever leave that thing?"

"Not really. How are you Semyonov?"

"I don't know. I need Stierlitz."

"What has he done?"

"He's deserted."

The Worker hissed through his teeth. "Maybe he just found another handler, boss-man. Maybe he's in deep cover."

"The Kremlin would know. He isn't. He's deserted."

"Why call me?"

"I want you to help me find him."

Semyonov leaned back into his chair in the private jet. The Worker was smoking his hookah across from him. Outside, the Pacific ocean.

I've done this before, thought Semyonov.

"Yes you have," said The Worker.

The hookah filled the small jet with smoke. Semyonov relaxed back into a private dream.

In it, he was a cavalryman, hacking with his sword through the enemy.

He felt strangely like a tree too, like his arm and his sword and the enemy were the same branch, swaying in the breeze.

The liquid light over the steepes was bronze, like his skin.

When he awoke they were touching down in Los Angeles. The Worker was making a phone call.

"I've arranged camels for us, to go into the desert."

Semyonov nodded. He hated camels.

For every Stierlitz, a nation. And for every Stierlitz, a thousand nations. We tumble in his regard, leaves.

Of the story.

Max?

" ... "

Max, are you there?

Max ventures into the black night. Who shall return from there, I cannot say.

I want to make it easier for you, Max!

" ... fuck ... you ..."

Be careful, Max!

Over the desert, lightning.

Inside his heart, oblivion. Inside oblivion, some fond regard. A music. A tune, to guide him through, playing in his heart. He smiles, in darkness.

It's not just about Russia, Max!

" ... yes it is ..."

It's about more than Russia!

... he's gone. I can only see a black storm over the desert.

Max. I'm sorry Max. I want to give you so much. The Russia you want. The Russia of your dreams. I want to build a whole new society for you. Whatever you want, Max.

But it won't be what I wanted to give you, Max. I'm afraid of that. It will be something else. Something you need. I don't know what.

Stay together in the darkness, Max. There's a lot

in there. Stay together!

" ... fuck ... you ..."

Max Stierlitz in the Desert

I am Max Stierlitz and this is my record. I am being written by an American spy, an enemy of Russia. Nevertheless, I live, and breathe, having taken refuge in a dimensional porthole through the help of one of my countrymen, an old woman who calls herself Baba Yaga.

There are many regrets I have in life, none more than my mistreatment of my kind mistress, Ekaterina. I wish that I could speak to her now. But I know it is not wise. Where I am now is not a safe place. It is not necessarily a bad place, but dangerous.

I am swallowed by complete darkness. All I can hear is my own breathing, and the wind.

I imagine this American spy, Dunn, must be so amused by my suffering. He must laugh at the evils he thrusts at me. He must be a sadist.

This is all right. In the KGB they teach us how to deal with sadists: wait them out. Eventually they will grow tired. Then they will grow weak. One might even be able to defeat them with kindness.

- Rabinovich, you know that we move towards communism. Why do you need so much money?
- What about the way back?

-- traditional Russian joke

...

Stierlitz Arrives

Again Stierlitz arrives. Arrives again, again.
Rearrives in himself, his body a tool of events
beyond his control, any whispered murder, any
bold plan, and terrible despair, all of it, rearrived
again, rearrived again, a thousand times, in the
dark.

We can't know what Stierlitz wants, we can only
guess – perhaps he himself does not know. Perhaps he is desperate to discover something. He is
a spy, after all.

What is it, Stierlitz? What are you after?

" ... hmm ..."

Tell me, Stierlitz, I need to know.

" ... hmm ..."

Goddamn it Stierlitz. To hell with you.

Stierlitz is invincible. He is unstoppable. Big
Russian Man. Brawny Soviet-era beast. Putin's
hero, Stierlitz! You are Putin's hero!

"Pushkin?"

Never mind, Stierlitz. You are bold and beautiful and in darkness. Eternal, like aspect of the sky.

A nebula, say, waiting to be born as a sun ...

"I think ... I should go ..."

Go then, Stierlitz. There are other worlds than these.

"These voices in my head ... driving me mad ..."

Tell us what it is, Stierlitz. Tell us what you feel.

"Escorted in the night. By the guards. They took me into the factory. I thought they were going to shoot me. It was dark, not quite morning. The dust hung in the air, and I heard a song in my head I hadn't heard since I was a boy, a little rhyme ...

"The phone call came and I was released on diplomatic grounds. Some goddamned Romanian backwater. I still remember the feeling in the air ... like death was the most beautiful thing that existed ...

"When I returned to Moscow, I met my wife. That summer."

Move darker into the darkness, Stierlitz. Lie back on the couch, it's okay. Defeat all your enemies. Within your mind.

" ... hummmmmmmmmmmm ..."

Meditating, Stierlitz?

" ... hummmmmmmmmmmmm ..."

Kill the beast within you, Stierlitz. Tame yourself. Break that bear.

"I will not."

Break that bear, Stierlitz.

"No."

Do it.

163

"Arrghk!"

The darkness is safe. Home. Infinite. Rotund. Malleable. Alive.

"Arrrrrrrrrrgh!"

What is it, Stierlitz?

"I see a light."

What is it?

"It is Moscow."

What is it doing, Stierlitz?

"Glowing."

Why, Stierlitz?

"It's growing brighter."

What now, Stierlitz?

"I'm going into it."

You'll be a ghost, Stierlitz.

"So be it."

...
In Moscow

Luminescent fields of buildings shimmer about him, like bright mushrooms in a midnight forest. His own limbs are translucent.

Above him, the sky is alive. Musically alive like a tidal pool, swirling with colored life, fuchsia and Cherokee red, charcoal and burnt yellows, indigo night. His beating heart shoots light down his veins, readouts of some galactic frequency. He opens his mouth to sigh,

[don't speak Stierlitz]

he closes his mouth. He is a ghost; he should be silent. Better not to terrify the people of Moscow, used to ghosts though they are.

Over the houses, musical light in dappled splashes, paintings of gods so brilliant and close by, making themselves and available to Stierlitz, and to us. The skies of evening over Moscow are frighteningly alive—much more frightening to Stierlitz than his new transparent body—he is, after all, a spook.

Their colors shift and swirl, lighting up his face with weird lights, as he walks down his old street.

His wife is at their door, looking down the street, with her sad face. Almost Stierlitz thinks thinks she sees him—she senses him but does not see him.

He stretches out his hand to touch her face, his

hand casts colored shadows on her cheek.

She turns, and goes in. He slips after her, stepping around her as she shuts their door.

He walks up the stairs.

Into the kitchen.

There is a man sitting there. Also KGB, with his long face.

She enters their kitchen.

"Max is gone," she says. "You know that."

"But we do not have proof," the man says.

How can Stierlitz not know this spy? It must be someone the zombie Stalin hired while he was still alive — and employee out of official channels. But no ... the man's face rings a faint bell ...

"We lost touch with Stierlitz in the American desert," the man says. "He was eaten by snakes."

"Ridiculous."

"Have you had any contact with him?"

"First you tell me he is dead. Then you ask me if I've heard from him. I don't believe in ghosts, officer."

"We have reason to believe Colonel Stierlitz contacted an extraterrestrial power."

His wife's laugh was beautiful. How he'd been missing it! He stood behind her chair, inhaling the scent of her hair. He watched the spy's face. Stierlitz was getting old—his memory for faces, at the academy and after, had been impeccable.

His wife poured the man tea.

"Thank you," he said, and drank.

His wife, and Stierlitz, watched him. Stierlitz

felt so close to her, though he was worlds away.

"Let me tell you a story," the man said. "The Russian Space Program recently launched several vessels to explore our solar system. Perhaps you saw it on the news. Three launches were official, and scheduled. One was not.

"Colonel Stierlitz was seen at Baikonur launch station shortly before this unofficial craft's launch.

"Of course, we will search your flat if necessary. But I would like to know if your husband mentioned anything to you about his plans. Or mentioned anything at all unusual that might assist us."

"My husband is loyal to Russia, sir. More loyal than you. Whatever he has done, it has been in service to Russia."

"You may well be right, Madame."

"I am right."

"So can you remember anything?"

"My husband was well after his mission to America. This you know. In my visit to him at hospital he mentioned he had been having strange dreams, which had never plagued him before. One dream in particular concerned Stalin. Our former Emperor."

"Comrade Stalin?" said the man, visibly uncomfortable.

"Emperor Stalin, yes, in the dream. He wore a miter on his head, like a Church Father. He drank blood."

"I see."

"Perhaps it is Stalin you should be looking for."
"Stalin is dead, Madame."

Moscow, of light and dark. We do not understand light. Any more than we understand god. Stierlitz humbled himself before his city, bowing like a penitent before the streaming vortex of color that was Moscow.

At Red Square he saw the girl who'd spoken to him there—however long ago that now was—her hands streaming light behind them like phosphorescent plankton in the sea. It was not the Moscow he knew, but it was close. Behind the city he had known all his life, within it. What tale, a haunting? What are its necessities?

The bound city so heavy for him, even heavier now that he is a ghost, he follows the man who interrogated his wife, into the same bar Stierlitz had frequented.

He watches the man drink. The sounds come to Stierlitz as though from far away. The light as through silk.

Stierlitz opens his mouth to speak.

[be silent Stierlitz]

He does not speak. The man finishes his vodka and goes out into the street.

It's darker now, the colors midnight. The pallette ash. Shades shifting and shifting. Moving over the midnight soil of the city. Moving through time a terrible movement, a centennial movement, thorough and dynamic, a terrible urgency in the light of the city, without pressure, without end, without agreement, without endorsement, without compensation, turgid with meaning.

Stierlitz opens his mouth to speak
a hum escapes him
hummmmmmmmmmmmmmmmm
hummmmmmmmmmmmmm
hummmmmmm

...

Ghosts of Moscow present and future

In the city of dreaming light, Moscow:

Before Stierlitz a trap door opened and he went down into it.

Two beasts appeared on his shoudlers, furry beasts with wings, resting on his shoulders as he descended the spiral stairs into the belly of Moscow.

"We're the ghosts of Moscow present and future," they said.

Into and down, around

Into, and down, around, inside and down within:

No one may tell of this symphony. No one may reveal its essence. No one may shout its name, or chant its low voice, give meaning to its nameless shape or shift and shoal its roll of the earth:

Now Stierlitz, tell us: what is it?

Stierlitz: "I am a man. As such, my knowledge is almost nothing. What the fuck are these things on my shoudlers for instance?"

The birds: "We already told you that."

Stierlitz: "There is little I can know and so my goal must remain the same. To defend the Republic."

"Is Russia a republic?"

Stierlitz: "Well, a Federation."

Who is it, who is it, Stierlitz, we told you so, we told you so Stierlitz, we told you so, who is it? Who shall it be, stierlitz? Who shall it be? Who shall it be, Stierlitz, who is . . .

Who is, Stierlitz?

"What is the question."

Save us, Stierlitz. Save us, you crazy warrior.

"I do the best I can. God knows I'm hardly up to the task. Tell me, do you know what I face?"

I don't Stierlitz. I wish I did.

"I am up against you. You are a horrible person. Well-meaning, perhaps, but horrible. What have you done to my Moscow?"

I didn't mean to, Stierlitz.

"I have to fix all the mucking about you've done. With these goddamned furry ghost birds on my shoudlers."

Yes, Stierlitz. Fix it, Stierlitz.

"God damn it."

"Sometimes you dream strange dreams, impossible and unnatural; you wake up and remember them clearly, and are surprised at a strange fact: you remember first of all that reason did not abandon you during the whole course of your dream; you even remember that you acted extremely cleverly and logically for that whole long, long time when you were surrounded by murderers, when they were being clever with you, concealed their intentions, treated you in a friendly way, though they already had their weapons ready and were only waiting for some sort of sign; you remember how cleverly you finally deceived them, hid from them; then you realize that they know your whole deception by heart and merely do not show you that they know where you are hiding; but you are clever and deceive them again—all that you remember clearly. But why at the same time could your reason be reconciled with such obvious absurdities and impossibilities, with which, among other things, your dream was filled? Before your eyes, one of your murderers turned into a woman, and from a woman into a clever, nasty little dwarf—and all that you allowed at once, as an accomplished fact, almost without the least perplexity, and precisely at the moment when, on the other hand, your reason was strained to the utmost, displaying extraordinary force, cleverness, keenness, logic? Why, also, on awakening from your dream and entering fully into reality, do you feel almost every time, and occasionally with an extraordinary force of impressions, that along with *the dream you are leaving behind something you have failed to fathom? You smile at the absurdity of your dream and feel at the same time that the tissue of those absurdities contains some thought, but a thought that is real, something that belongs to your true life, something that exists and has always existed in your heart; it is as if your dream has told you something new, prophetic, awaited; your impression is strong, it is joyful or tormenting, but what it is and what has been told you—all that you can neither comprehend nor recall."*

Fyodor Dostoyevsky, *The Idiot*

Part 5
Moscow

50
The little girl

Stierlitz runs into the dark. Over him other birds are flapping. The mutant birds on his shoulders fly up with them into the dark, cheering Stierlitz on, rooting him on, crying and laughing in the dark dungeon air.

The girl from the square is there. She leads him into a library, with a candle.

They sit, and eat bread. She watches him.

She swallows the bread.

"What is happening to me?" he asks her.

"You're being released," she says.

"Released from what?"

"From life."

"You mean I'm dead?" Stierlitz almost chokes on his bread.

"Not quite yet, Stierlitz. But I'm here to tell you, that if you would live, you must try even harder. Stierlitz, Stalin is still alive. He's still alive down here. He cannot die."

"He's alive again?" asked Stierlitz.

"He's alive again Stierlitz. Save us, won't you?"

"Yes, Mademoiselle."

He rises and takes his leave of the demoiselle and straightens his coat and oils his firearm, standing in the candlelight.

Ahead of him he can hear the birds flapping and he goes down to meet them, into the canals, and the bird shit, and the dark.

We can flash and we can chant. We can move and we can dance. We can flashchant and move-dance. Eh, Stierlitz?

"Hummmmmmmmmmmmm."

The canal moves deeper in. To the canal zone.

To the fires within Moscow.

To its hopes and dreams.

In Moscow's dark heart, the future.

Stierlitz holds his gun in his hands. He thinks of his women. He fantasizes of taking them to bed together, something he knows will never happen.

Up ahead, he can see his old friend, the musician.

"Friend! Come aboard. You look lost."

The man climbs aboard. His fiddle is broken.

"My instrument," the man says.

"I'm sorry," says Stierlitz. "Would you like me to take you back, to the surface?"

"No. I'm all right here. Thank you for stopping for me."

"Of course."

Stierlitz continues to row, and the man sings a song in Russian, about a winter girl who fell asleep, and could not wake up.

Can not, can not wake up, Stierlitz, no matter how hard you try. The sleep of Russia is eternal. Longer than this earth.

Longer than this Earth in my long goodbye, Stierlitz, the sleep of Russia is your own, so musical and unafriad. Tell me, Stierlitz, will you be brave when you kill Stalin?

Stierlitz nods, rowing.

Will you defeat him forever?

Stierlitz is silent.

Tell me, Stierlitz. What can you do against this evil?

Stierlitz is rowing.

Rowing into the wilderness.

Into our heart.

Stierlitz, tell me, what is it with you? Why did you charm Putin so? Why did you do that, Stierlitz? A mad thing to do.

"Pushkin was dead long before my time, young man."

Ha ha ha!

Stierlitz, Stalin is approaching.

He loads his weapon.

The musician tunes his instrument.

Stalin is singing.

Like a wasp in the dark.

Like a lover in death.

Like a killer.

Like a god.

Sing, Stalin!

. . .

I AM STALIN!

51
Stalin Sings

I AM STALIN!

MY DESTINY IS A DREAM.

ALL THESE YEARS, I'VE BEEN DREAMING. DREAMING! OF DEATH!

DREAMING OF DEATH IN MOSCOW!

DREAMING . . .

MY WOMAN AND MY CHILD ARE WITH ME IN THE DARK.

I DREAM OF THEM!

I DREAM OF DEATH IN MOSCOW IN THE SILENT FORESTS AND THE SILENT ISLES. I DREAM OF MY MUSIC, A SYMPHONY OF NIGHT.

I EAT THE FLESH OF BIRDS AND I AM SILENT.

[the birds are flapping their wings over the canal]

[Stierlitz squints into the darkness, pointing his gun]

I SING MY SYMPHONY OF NIGHT!

I AM BROKEN THINGS AND HARSH MUSIC.

I AM YOUR DREAM.

I AM YOUR DREAM.

I AM YOUR DREAM, STIERLITZ.

DREAM WITH ME, OF DEATH.

DREAM WITH ME OF DEATH AND I WILL TAKE YOU WITH ME, TO WHERE THE CHANTING STOPS, TO WHERE THE LIGHT MAKES NO

ACCORD, AND WE CAN BE TOGETHER IN THE
DARKEST LIGHT, THE MUSICAL AND DARK-
EST LIGHT BEYOND THE SEA. BEYOND ALL
SEAS.

LET ME TAKE YOU WITH ME.

LET ME HAVE YOU STIERLITZ.

[Stierlitz fires his weapon.]

[There is a splash.]

[But is only a crow, with strange eyes, dead.]

[The birds of night alight on Stierlitz's shoulders. The musician stops his tune.]

"Only a bird, Stierlitz?" asks the musician.

Stierlitz strokes the dead bird's head.

"I'm sorry, little man," he says.

Three men are sitting in a cell in Dzerzhinsky Square. The first asks the second why he has been imprisoned, who replies, "Because I criticized Karl Radek." The first man responds, "But I am here because I spoke out in favor of Radek!" They turn to the third man who has been sitting quietly in the back, and ask him why he is in jail. He answers, "I'm Karl Radek."

-- traditional Russian joke

52

Moscow

Stierlitz is being served tea. There has been a reorganization of the KGB, and he has been put on temporary leave, which he does not like.

He sips his tea by Red Square, watching the dawn colors fade from the sky.

Inside the tea is a note.

"Meet me tonight. Kat."

What do you remember, Stierlitz? Is it enough? Tell me, Stierlitz. I want to know!

Stierlitz pays for his tea and walks through the square, watching the light. He would like a drink but it is too early. He's been drinking too much.

Everything in Moscow is too close, suddenly. He hops on the tram, headed to the edge of the city. To the trees.

At the last tram stop he buys a sandwich and walks into the forest.

"Stierlitz. I was looking for you," says The Worker, hopping down from his tree.

"Worker! I didn't know you were back in town."

"Yes. Stierlitz, there is something I must tell you. You may be in danger."

"I am always in danger," said Stierlitz. "That is my job."

The Worker popped a blue mushroom into his mouth.

"Stierlitz. This is a threat from within your organization. It is my duty to warn you. Semyonov no longer trusts you."

"Sometimes I no longer trust myself."

"I'll help you if I can, Stierlitz. Tell me what I can do."

"Just be yourself, Worker. That's all."

The men shook hands and The Worker climbed back into his tree. Stierlitz continued on his walk. His mistress would be waiting for him.

But all that he had done . . . it disconcerted even him. To undertake such great struggles for Mother Russia surely changed her. He did not know quite who She was anymore.

In his mind's eye he could still see the ship . . . curling over the alien horizon . . . with the beast beneath him, warm, and friendly, and far away.

Stierlitz is dancing.

What who when dancing.

What who when dancing, in the earth, and over it, within it.

Within the earth, a man.

Within the man, the earth.

Dance with me, Stierlitz.

Dance with me over your light:

The Russians are a dancing people. And beautiful. But what torment came lodged within them, Stierlitz?

I want to know!

But he is dancing.

Beneath the eaves of the trees. The Worker watches.

Stierlitz walks back into the city, his body humming.

He makes love to Ekaterina, in the moonlight.

Outside, Russia is sleeping.

Inside, Russia is awake.

Something is different.

The crow is at his window.

"Crow," says Stierlitz.

"Kraak!" says the crow.

"I'm sorry, crow."

"Kraak!" says the crow.

He gives it a piece of bread. The bird eats it, and watches Stierlitz, its head cocked.

"Russia is waking up again," says Stierlitz.

"Kraak!"

"I'll need your help."

53
Russia awakes

Revolution come again, bloodless as midnight, more beautiful than a sunrise, the crowds.

Colorless the crowds, black white midnight bodies, storming all fences.

Storming all fences of the heart.

Stierlitz is carried by them, victorious, on their shoulders. A hero.

Heroes are watching at the gates, over the fireside.

Heroes are watching in the trees.

Stierlitz is crying.

The KGB has been dismantled.

Stierlitz is unemployed.

His paltry pension—even that has evaporated.

The Russian state is no more. But the people have never been more joyful.

The Rus is dead.

Inside him Stierlitz can feel the frame of the longboat, its oars, and its keel.

Russia means "row." Moscow means "marsh."

Stierlitz means "Bull braid."

Over the shoulders of his people Stierlitz listens to the chanting, like a fine mantra.

What will he do?

Stalin covered the sky, screaming memories.

But only in Stierlitz's head.

The vokda bottle passed to his lips, and he drank. The little water of the little life, now eternity:

In his dreams, he slept. And in waking, he slept too. Waiting for the moment.

Ekaterina bore him a son. Who he named Star. And he taught him the banjo, the funny music of his boyhood.

No one shall call Stierlitz now.

Bull braid is retired.

The phone shall not ring.

Nor shall Semyonov heed his bright call, to go to the breech.

Go to the breech, Semyonov, grin between your teeth, and take up the symphony, of revolution . . .

Russia is a dream. Stierlitz is a king. Not red, but grey.

Grey King, what shadows sleeping bide thee, on thy long march into the reeds?

Pray, tell us so, and we will shape for thee a moniker, to bond thee to all the waves.

Come, let us launch thee, burning, into the sea:

Acknowledgments

I am grateful to Dan Souder at *The Brasilia Review*, and Casey Dorman at *The Lost Coast Review*, who published early chapters of this work. I am grateful too to Anatoly Belilovsky, who was an enthusasitic early reader, and sharp, generous critic.

Of course I am invaluably indebted to Yulian Semyonov, whose character Maxim Maximovich Isayev I have shamelessly kidnapped and thrust into my parallel universe. Whether I have done Bull Braid sufficient honor is not something I can judge.

Again I am indebted to the incomparable Barbara Sobczyńska, who has kindly drawn the cover for this book. Her sensibilities from her capital at Krakow continue to provide me with much needed inspiration.

In some ways I feel the United States is headed into a kind of Soviet-era Eastern European malaise. Perhaps Max Stierlitz may yet be able to help us escape.

About the author

Robin Wyatt Dunn was born in Wyoming in 1979. He writes and teaches in Los Angeles.

Made in the USA
San Bernardino, CA
09 April 2016